THE JINX

Heartthrob Hospital Book 2

LORI WILDE

D1715078

CeeCee Adams was cursed. Hexed. Jinxed. Doomed.

Forever unlucky in love and destined to traipse the earth as a single woman, compliments of the Jessup family whammy.

How else to explain the numerous failed marriages and hapless love affairs among the women in her family? How else could she account for the likes of Lars Vandergrin, a six-foot-four Neanderthal who wrestled for the WWF?

Lars had a grin to melt snow off mountain peaks, sheer blond hair cascading to his waist, and hands as grabby as quadruplet two-year-olds at a grocery store. The man also possessed the same rudimentary disregard for the word "no" as the aforementioned toddlers. For the last three hours she'd fended off his advances while sitting through the latest high-octane action-adventure flick, and she was quickly running out of patience.

Thanks a million, Grandma Addie, as if dating in this new millennium wasn't difficult enough.

Fifty years ago, back in the old country, her maternal grandmother, Addie Jessup, had stolen a fortuneteller's lover. The fortuneteller, a rather vengeful sort it seems, not only zapped Addie with the evil eye, but damned every Jessup female for three generations. No woman in Addie's direct lineage stayed married and divorce was as commonplace as swapping cars.

Which was the very reason CeeCee never dated any guy for too long. She refused to fall into the same trap as her mother, aunts, and older sister, Geena. No multiple marriages for her. No revolving charge account at bridal registries. No ugly child custody battles.

No, siree. She was forever a free spirit. Single and loving it.

Except for times like these.

She'd met Lars when he had sought treatment in her physical therapy department for a torn rotator cuff. Over the past three weeks he had pestered her to go out with him. She had finally agreed, hoping to persuade him to appear in the wrestling regalia he wore as the Missing Link for St. Madeleine Hospital's charity bachelor auction held annually the third Friday in July. The auction raised healthcare funds for Houston's inner-city kids and having been one of those kids, it was a cause that held CeeCee's heart.

At the moment she and Lars were standing beneath the porch lamp on the front stoop of her apartment. Lars had her pinned against the door, his hot breath fanning the hairs along her forehead, fingers thick as kielbasa twisting the top button of her blouse. She cared deeply about the charity auction but not deeply enough to grant this slab of marble carte blanche access to her body.

"Stop it." She swatted his hand and her charm bracelet jangled. "I don't appreciate being pawed."

"Come on, *bay-bee,* you owe me." He puckered his lips.

"Owe you? How do you figure?"

"Shrimp dinner, movie, popcorn."

"Hang on, I'll give you the cash."

"No cash." He shook his head and his hair swung like the blond mane on the My Little Pony her first stepfather had given her for her seventh birthday. "The Missing Link wants kissy-kissy."

"If you don't remove your hands from my body this instant, you'll be singing soprano."

He giggled and ground his hips against her. "You're feisty. Lars like that."

He'd been referring to himself in the third person all night.

"You haven't seen feisty, buster. Hands off." She didn't intimidate easily, but a small splash of fear rippled through her. Lars was a very large man.

Immediately she thought of her good friend and next-door neighbor, Dr. Jack Travis. Was Jack home?

She dodged Lars' attempt to kiss her and shot a glance through the sweltering June darkness to the ground floor apartment across the courtyard. Light slanted through the blinds.

At that moment she would have given anything to be with good old dependable Jack, listening to jazz music, sharing a laugh. Jack had such a great laugh. A resonant sound that made her feel safe, secure, and cared for. She valued their platonic relationship far more than he would ever know.

If things got really nasty, she would scream for Jack, but she wouldn't call unless she had no choice. She proudly fought her own battles. Besides, thanks to the curse, she'd had more than her share of run-ins with guys like Lars. Still, it was nice knowing she had Jack as backup.

"Come on, *bay-bee*." Lars cupped his palm against her nape. "Let's go inside."

Over my dead body!

"Listen here, Vandergrin." She splayed a palm across his chest and cocked her knee, ready to use it if necessary. "Things are moving too fast between us."

"You want me in your bachelor auction? I do a favor for you. You do a favor for me."

Blackmailer.

This time she wasn't quick enough. Lars captured her mouth and gave her a hard, insistent kiss. She was in trouble. Forget subtlety. No more Ms. Nice Girl. As for the charity auction, she'd just have to find another celebrity.

"Shove off!" CeeCee jerked her mouth away at the same moment Lars thrust out his tongue. Her forehead accidentally whacked into his chin.

"Yeow," he screamed and pressed a hand to his mouth. "You made me bwite my tonwue!"

<hr>

"THANK YOU FOR TAKING OUT MY GARBAGE." Miss Abercrombie smiled at Jack.

The elderly lady, who had once been an exotic dancer and had numerous photographs displayed around her apartment to prove it, wore a blue-green muumuu with a bright-pink feather boa draped around her neck. She wobbled on three-inch mules and peered at him over the top of her soda-bottle-thick glasses. In her arms she held a snow-white poodle dubbed Muffin. The dog's curly coat was festooned with pink bows, and her toenails were painted to match.

"It's no problem." He picked up the trash bag and headed for the door.

Miss Abercrombie *clip-clomped* behind him.

Every Sunday night that he wasn't on duty at the hospital, Jack took out the trash for the elderly single women at the River Run apartment complex and for one other special lady as well. His next-door neighbor and best friend, CeeCee Adams.

At the thought of CeeCee, he smiled. Zany, bubbly, flame haired CeeCee with her fearless zest for adventure and her unbridled lust for life. He admired everything about her and wished he could be more like her.

Muffin whined from her owner's embrace.

"She wants to come with you," Miss Abercrombie said. "Do you mind?"

The button-eyed mutt gazed longingly at him and wriggled from Miss Abercrombie's grasp. Tail wagging, Muffin leaped to the ground and sniffed his ankle.

"I can't believe how much Muffin loves you. She

usually hates men. Then again, you're not like most men, are you. You're so sweet."

Yeah. So women kept telling him. But sweetness and a two-dollar bill wouldn't even buy him a cup of decaf latte at the coffee shop around the corner.

"Come on, Muff." He would have preferred not to have the dog snaking between his legs on his trek to the dumpster.

He and the poodle stopped at the bottom of the stairs to pick up two other garbage sacks Jack had left behind before climbing the stairs to Miss Abercrombie's apartment. Prince, the border collie who guarded apartment 112, jumped to his feet and trotted after them. As they rounded the corner, a roly-poly beagle/terrier cross waddled from the alley and joined the procession.

Terrific. Not only was he the neighborhood trash collector, it seemed he was now the official dog walker as well.

He caught his breath as they neared CeeCee's apartment and his pulse revved. He hadn't seen her for a couple of days, and he missed her.

A lot.

From the moment he'd first seen her sailing through the courtyard on in-line skates, a saucy, come-catch-me-big-boy smile on her oval face, her curly red hair streaking behind her like livid fire, he'd wanted her.

He'd known he wasn't her type, and he had never once rallied the courage to tell her how he felt. How could he? Dr. Jack was solid, responsible, dependable.

Face it, he was boring.

He saw the men she dated; scuba divers and rock climbers, bungee jumpers and snowboarders. Guys with tattoos and pierced body parts, long hair and beard stubble. Men who stared danger in the face and laughed.

Men like his twin brother, Zack.

For identical twins, their differences were amazing. Jack was cautious; Zack reckless. Jack methodical; Zack messy. Jack dedicated his life to medicine. Zack, a famous motocross champion, dedicated his life to wine, women, and wheels. Most women considered Jack a great friend. Those same women considered Zack a great lover.

He wasn't jealous. Well, not much.

Occasionally, however, he would have given anything to possess Zack's charm with the ladies. Like when CeeCee came over to his apartment, flopped on his sofa, tucked those pinup quality legs beneath her, and filled his ears with another tale of relationship woes.

If she'd asked him for his opinion, he could have

told her where she was making her mistakes. The guys she picked were wrong for her. A spontaneous woman like CeeCee needed a steady guy to balance her out. Someone like himself. But he was too afraid of ruining their friendship to offer unsolicited advice.

He started up the staircase. A guttural scream from the direction of CeeCee's apartment stopped him cold. He sprang into action, sprinting the remaining steps to the second-floor landing. He spotted CeeCee standing on her doorstep grappling with a human rendition of King Kong's third cousin.

"Let go!" She tried to yank her arm from the big ape's grip.

The primate wore black leather motorcycle pants and hobnailed boots and chains. He towered at least six foot three and possessed the prominent brow of a Cro-Magnon. His platinum-blond hair dangled to his butt, and he had one hand clamped over her mouth.

Despite being four inches shorter and at least sixty pounds lighter, Jack never hesitated. His best friend was in trouble.

He slung the trash bags to the ground, lowered his head, and plowed into the guy's abdomen at a dead run.

Jack hit him hard.

The Granite Mountain's stomach muscles were solid as bone. The creature didn't even grunt.

Jack heard birds singing. *Tweet. Tweet. Tweet.* His knees slid to the cement.

Uh-oh.

Granite Mountain sort of growled, shook his head, grabbed Jack by the collar, and pulled him to his feet. His long hair slapped Jack in the face, stinging his eyes.

Jack's chin snapped up, and he looked into a kisser as deadly as a steel trap, and he knew he'd met his Waterloo.

Fools rush in.

Which was the very reason he rarely acted heedlessly. He should have been smart and telephoned the cops. But he hadn't thought. He'd seen CeeCee was in trouble and he had simply acted.

A first for Jack Travis. In a weird way, despite the peril, he kind of enjoyed his automatic, yet foolhardy bravery.

"CeeCee," Jack managed over looking at the business end of a fist the size of a Virginia ham. "Are you all right?"

"Is *she* aw wright?" Granite Mountain howled. "She de one who made me bwite my tonwue."

"I'm sure you deserved it." Jack's gaze flicked to CeeCee. She looked gorgeous in skintight capri leggings and a form-fitting rainbow-colored tunic blouse.

"She's a witch," Granite Mountain snarled.

"Apologize." Jack thrust out his chest and faced the guy down.

"What are you gonna do about it, twash boy?" Granite Mountain planted a hand on Jack's chest and gave him a shove. Jack stumbled backward into the garbage sacks.

Calm fury overtook him. Never in his life had he been so determined. The creature was going to apologize to CeeCee if it was the last thing he ever did.

Jack picked up a trash bag and swung it at man. "I'm going to kick your backside around this apartment complex. That's what I'm going to do about it."

"Oh, yeah?"

"Yeah." Jack smacked the dude in the chest with a trash bag.

The bag split open, splattering garbage over the man's leather ensemble. He let out an angry whoop and lunged for Jack, trapping his neck in a stranglehold and squeezing like a starving boa constrictor.

"Don't you dare hurt him, Lars!" CeeCee commanded the iron giant. "Let him go! Now!"

Lars, of course that was his name. A Viking. Stars burst behind Jack's eyelids. Red. Yellow. White. His head swam dizzily. He heard dogs yapping, but they sounded very far off.

If he didn't do something quickly, he was going to

pass out, leaving CeeCee at the mercy of this cretin. Reaching out, he snatched a handful of long blond hair.

And jerked with all his might.

"Ow! Stwop pulling my hair," Lars howled.

Jack tugged harder.

Lars spun to the left, and his elbow wrapped around Jack's neck. Both of Jack's fists were entangled in Lars' mane.

CeeCee bound into action. Faster than Wonder Woman in a tailspin, she lunged onto the man's back.

For one crazy, dizzy moment the three of them were locked in a bizarre tango. Lars staggered forward, then back, trying to maintain his balance with CeeCee above him, Jack beneath his feet.

"Let him go!" CeeCee shouted.

"Make him wet go of me," Lars bawled.

Muffin, Prince, and the beagle-terrier mix barked and chased around them in a circle.

"Everybody let go of everybody," Jack choked out.

Throughout the apartment complex doors were opening. People shouted. An audience gathered in the courtyard. More dogs scaled the stairs and joined the fray.

Lars spun into the wall, trying to dislodge CeeCee who still clung to his back. In the process, his grip on Jack's neck loosened.

Jack released Lars' hair and instead reached for his ankles, intending on tripping him.

"Jump off, CeeCee."

"He's the Missing Link."

"Tell me about it. He's a cross between King Kong and a heavy weight boxer."

"No, you don't understand. He's Lars Vandergrin, a professional wrestler, Jack."

"Oops. Now you tell me."

Lars growled.

"Jump. I swear he's going down," Jack urged, determined to remain resolute despite the fact he was tangling with a professional wrestler. He kept his hands locked like handcuffs around the man's ankles.

CeeCee cleared Lars' back at the same moment the man tumbled like a felled redwood straight into the pile of trash sacks torn open during the fight.

Slam dunk!

Lars hit with a thud. The staircase shook. He lay lifeless in the debris.

Jack and CeeCee stared at each other.

"Is he breathing?" She squinted. "Oh my gosh, did we kill him?"

Pulse pounding at the thought he might have hurt a fellow human being, Jack hurried forward to investigate, prepared to do CPR if necessary.

"*Oof.*" Lars groaned. He sat up and slowly shook

his head with the lethargic motion of a hibernating bear rousing from a long winter's nap.

Jack backed away with his hands raised. "Let's have no more trouble."

Lars looked down. Peanut butter and coffee grounds hung in his hair. Something green and sticky oozed from his elbow. Eggshells decorated his lap. A banana peel dangled from one ear. Muffin licked the toe of his boot. The other dogs were sniffing hungrily at his clothes.

"My hair! I just washed it." Lars burst into tears.

"Gee," CeeCee muttered, standing on tiptoes to peer over Jack's shoulder. "What a big baby."

Muffin looked up at Lars and growled.

"Poodles!" Lars cried. "I hate poodles." The huge man lumbered to his feet and took off.

The yelping dogs gave chase, nipping at the Missing Link's heels as he thundered down the stairs. *Woof, woof, woof.*

Jack and CeeCee leaned over the railing, watching the Missing Link screech away into the inky darkness, then turned to smile at each other.

The neighbors who had gathered during the altercation, applauded and cheered before calling to their dogs and ambling back to their apartments, shaking their heads in amusement.

CeeCee flung her arms around Jack's neck. Her

gold charm bracelet jangled merrily in his ears. Her cheeks were flushed, her green eyes sparkling with excitement, her hair sexily mussed. Her well-rounded chest rose and fell heavily against his.

She smelled exquisite. Like rainbows and sunshine and moonbeams. Jack's stomach took a roller-coaster ride up to his throat and then plunged back down again. He realized he was holding his breath.

Waiting.

"My hero!" she exclaimed, then cupped his face in her hands and kissed him.

$$\text{🜲} \quad 2 \quad \text{🜲}$$

CeeCee couldn't say who was more stunned by her impromptu kiss, she or Jack.

She certainly hadn't planned on kissing him. A smart woman didn't go around kissing her best guy friend on the lips. Not if she intended to keep him as her friend, and she considered Jack's friendship one of her most prized possessions.

But what a Leonardo DiCaprio/Kate Winslet/*Titanic* sort of kiss it was! CeeCee sank as hard and fast as the ill-fated ocean liner.

Jack's clean-shaven cheeks were smooth against her palms, a pleasing contrast to the scruffy-faced men she normally dated. Driven by spontaneous impulse, she pressed her mouth to his in the heat of the moment, intending nothing more than a quick peck to thank him for rescuing her from Lars.

Instead, his mouth welcomed her warmly. She had allowed her eyelids to drift shut, her lips to part.

Blood strummed through her veins, pounding loudly in her ears. Her knees drooped like overcooked spaghetti. Her skin tingled as if she had sprinted a mile in under a minute flat.

Oh, she never wanted to stop.

In the course of the past five months she had touched Jack many times. She had brushed against his fingers reaching into the same popcorn bowl they shared while indulging in their mutual passion for *Monty Python* movies. She had patted his shoulder to comfort him when things had not gone well with one of his patients at the hospital. She had even taken his hand and helped him from his car in the bright sunlight and into his apartment after he'd had eye surgery to correct his nearsightedness.

While touching him in the past had been a pleasant experience, it had never raised the kind of feelings in her that kissing him did.

She wanted to keep on kissing him until the earth stopped spinning. Until the sun stopped rising and setting. Until birds stopped migrating and the polar ice caps melted like Popsicles in Arizona.

Holy cow, what was wrong with her?

She could not risk romantic involvement with Jack. Not now. Not ever. She was cursed. Any love affair could only end tragically, and she would never hurt him like that.

Ever.

He was too good for the likes of her. CeeCee's eyes flew open and she found herself staring deeply into Jack's startled eyes.

Instantly they broke apart and dropped their gazes, neither able to look at the other.

"Um... I'm sorry. I didn't mean... I got carried away." CeeCee lightly fingered her sizzling lips, both amazed and terrified at what had just transpired between them.

What had she done? Without intending to do so, she'd caused a gigantic shift in their relationship.

"You took me by surprise," Jack admitted, a good-natured smile flitting across his lips. "But it was a very nice surprise."

"Whew." She focused her gaze on the garbage strewn across the upstairs landing. Her next words were very important. She had to treat the kiss casually, as if it meant absolutely nothing.

"Whew, indeed."

"What a mess. I'll find fresh garbage bags and help you clean up."

He reached out a hand and lightly encircled her wrist with his fingers. "Forget the garbage for now. I think we should talk about what just happened."

Nervously she laughed and pushed her free hand through her hair. His fingers burned like a brand against her skin. "You want to talk about Lars?"

"No," he said firmly. "I want to talk about you and me and that kiss."

CeeCee swallowed hard. "Let's not make a mountain out of a molehill. It was just a 'thank-you' kiss."

"It felt like much more to me."

"Please, Jack," she begged.

She didn't want things to change between them. If she admitted she'd experienced something monumental when their lips met, then he would want more. She knew Jack. Whenever he fixed his mind on something he wanted, he never let go until he got it.

"Please, what, CeeCee?" His voice was husky, his body tense.

"Let's forget about the whole thing."

"I don't want to forget it."

The expression in his dark-brown eyes clearly said, *I want to be waaay more than friends with you.*

That look scared the bejesus out of her.

CeeCee cleared her throat. She couldn't have Jack believing they might have a romantic future together. Better to hurt his feelings a little now than to break his heart later.

Cruel to be kind, so the saying goes.

Opening her mouth, CeeCee told the biggest

whopper of her life. "I'm sorry to disappoint you, Jack, but it was like kissing my brother."

ॐ

LIKE KISSING HER BROTHER?!

Jack fumed to himself twenty minutes later after he'd disposed of the garbage and taken a cocky Muffin, complete with a hank of long blond hair triumphantly plucked from the Missing Link's head, back to Miss Abercrombie.

Apparently, the wrestler's poodle phobia had been well founded. Jack actually felt a little sorry for the guy. Muffin could be more protective than a pit bull.

He washed up in his bathroom and stared at himself in the mirror. How did CeeCee know what kissing a brother was like? She didn't even have a brother.

He studied his reflection. Okay, maybe he was a bit stodgy and maybe he didn't have the animal magnetism of the Missing Link, but to say kissing him was like kissing her brother.

Ouch! Low blow.

Plus, he knew she was lying.

He had felt her willing response. Her breathing had quickened; her lips had softened; her arms had gone around his neck. She had murmured deep in her throat like a contented kitten. Then, when she had told him the kiss had not affected her in the same way it had affected him, her cheeks had flushed tomato-red and she'd been unable to look him in the eyes.

Yep. She'd fibbed.

What he didn't know was why, but he was determined to find out.

Jack left his apartment, then stalked across the courtyard and up the stairs to her place. His palms were sweating, the voice in the back of his head shouting that he would screw up his friendship with CeeCee if he wasn't careful.

Jack took a deep breath and told the voice to take a hike. *Pretend you're Zack. What would your twin brother do?* He plastered a bedroom grin on his face, cocked his hips forward, and knocked on her door.

A long minute passed.

Do-do-do-do. Do-do-do. The theme song from final Jeopardy ran through his head as he waited, the emotional tension mounting.

He knocked again.

No answer.

Had she fallen asleep? He looked at his watch. Eleven o'clock. She had to be at work at seven in the morning. He couldn't blame her for going to bed. He should be considerate, head home, and save the discussion for tomorrow. He had an early surgical case himself.

He turned to leave, but something stopped him.

No, by God, he wasn't leaving this for tomorrow. He was tired of losing out on the good things in life.

Jack raised his hand to knock again and the door opened.

CeeCee peered out, hair turbaned in a towel. She was barefoot and wore a silky yellow caftan that melded to her curves like cling wrap.

His pulse skittered wildly.

"Sorry," she apologized and crinkled her cute little nose. "Just got out of the shower. I must look a fright."

"You look gorgeous."

Raising a hand to tuck a damp tendril of ginger-colored hair back up inside the turban, she snorted. "No makeup, hair in a towel. I don't think so."

She was a beautiful woman, yes, with a body that wouldn't quit. But he liked so many other wonderful things about her. He admired her inner fire, her lively spirit. Whenever he was near her, Jack felt like more of a man.

Tonight, he had reached a crossroads. He was sick of watching her date creeps. Sick of remaining silent waiting for her to notice him in a sexual way. His patience had run out.

A drop of water glistened on her cheek. Jack ached to reach out and whisk the droplet away.

Go ahead. Why not? It's what Zack would do.

And so he did.

CeeCee sucked in her breath at his touch and took a step backward. Instead of waiting for her to invite him inside as he normally would have, Jack breezed past her.

"Come on in," she said, closing the door behind them. "Have a seat. Would you like some iced tea?"

He nodded, not because he was thirsty but because he needed to have something to do with his hands...hands hankering to caress her.

"Be right back." She headed for the kitchen, stopping long enough to turn on the MP3 player. Strains of Duke Ellington filled the room. They had discovered on the first day they'd met that they both loved jazz.

Jack sank onto the couch.

CeeCee returned a minute later, handed him a glass of iced tea, then curled up beside him, tucking her legs beneath her in an unconsciously sexy manner. He couldn't pry his eyes off her, his gaze tracking her every movement.

How to start the conversation?

Not yet ready for the direct "Zack Attack"

approach, he took a sip of iced tea, then asked, "How did you cause Lars to bite his tongue?"

"I swear it was an accident." CeeCee chuckled. "But he shouldn't have been trying to shove the thing down my throat without my permission."

"Remind me never to get fresh with you."

"As if you would." She waved a hand, effectively dismissing him as any kind of threat. "You're much too honorable of a man to force yourself on a woman."

Her glibness bugged Jack. Did CeeCee actually consider him completely harmless, and was she really so clueless about his feelings for her? Powerful sexual feelings he barely managed to camouflage.

He shifted on the couch, looked her in the eyes, and asked her the question he'd been dying to ask her for five months. "All kidding aside, CeeCee, why do you keep going out with guys like Lars?"

"Lars wasn't a real date." She shrugged. "He's an ex-patient, and I was trying to convince him to appear at the hospital charity auction, not date him. Guess he's not gonna say yes now."

"Probably not."

"Damn. I promised the director I could secure a celebrity to help sell tickets. Maybe someday I'll learn to stop shooting my mouth off."

Tilting her head back, CeeCee took a swallow from her glass.

Jack's gaze melded to her throat. He couldn't seem to peel his stare from her slender, swanlike neck. His mouth watered; his stomach heated.

You shouldn't be having these lascivious feelings toward your best friend, his cautious voice urged. *Not if you want to keep her as your best friend.*

"Back on the subject," he said, ignoring his interfering conscience. Opportunity had knocked and he was flinging open the door. "I'll grant you that Lars wasn't your dream date and you weren't picturing settling down and making babies with him."

"Heaven forbid!"

"But you've definitely got a pattern going, CeeCee. What's the deal? Why do you keep picking emotionally immature men?"

"I'm just having fun." She shrugged.

"Why don't you go out with a nice, dependable guy?" Jack toyed with his glass.

A guy like me.

CeeCee rolled her eyes. "In a word? Nice guys are boring."

Her statement sliced his gut. She thought he was boring. He'd always suspected as much, but now he knew for sure.

"Present company excepted, of course," she said quickly.

But it was too late, he already knew what she thought of him. She wanted wild fun, a good time. Something he didn't think he could provide. Oh sure, he could pretend to be that guy for a little while, but it just wasn't his nature.

"Jackie." She leaned over and touched his hand.

Blistering white sparks shot through him, and it took every ounce of control he possessed to remain calm, cool, and collected.

"I appreciate your concern, I really do, but you don't have to worry about me. I can fend for myself. Honest."

"Like with Lars tonight?"

She pursed her lips. "He was an exception. Most guys aren't *that* pushy."

"Cee, if you keep going out with bad boys, how are you ever going to find a good man? One who'll cherish and respect you the way you deserve to be cherished and respected."

"That's the whole idea, Jack. I don't intend on getting married."

"Ever?"

She shook her head.

Dumbstruck, he could only stare. "But why not?"

"It's a long story." She sighed and waved a hand. He couldn't help admiring her long, shapely fingers.

"I've got two ears and all the time in the world. I want to know why a beautiful, vibrant young woman with so much to offer the right man never wants to marry."

"Swear you won't laugh at me?"

"Of course not."

"Okay. I suppose I do owe you an explanation, considering you've seen me through several miserable dates and rescued me from the Missing Link."

※

NERVOUSLY CEECEE TOOK A DEEP BREATH AND peeped at him through lowered lashes.

Jack sat up straight, not saying a word.

Every time she peeked over at him, she kept thinking about their kiss. Damn it! Jack was her friend and nothing else. She could not, would not let their relationship become anything more than platonic. For both their sakes. Her entire life she had trained herself not to expect much from the male sex. She knew from experience they couldn't be counted on in the tough times.

"Have fun with men," Gramma Addie had told her, "but don't think you can escape the curse."

She had learned to make the most of fate. In high school she'd been dubbed the girl most likely to break hearts. In college, her roomies had razzed her about putting in a revolving door for all her boyfriends. At the hospital, her colleagues believed her to be lighthearted and free-spirited and always up for a good time.

Essentially, she was all those things.

She'd striven to cultivate her adventuresome, no-holds-barred personality. She told jokes around the water cooler and regularly threw parties. She went out three or four nights a week, dancing, karaoke, hanging out with club bands. On weekends she liked to rent watercrafts or go to martial arts tournaments or ride in bike-a-thons.

Yet no one ever guessed that deep down inside she longed for something more.

Just once she'd like to be known as the quiet one or the smart one or the complex one. Not even her closest friends had the slightest clue she was secretly aching to be loved by a man who could promise her happily ever after.

But it wasn't going to happen, and she knew that. No man could promise her a rosy romance. There was no point pining for things she couldn't have. Melancholia wasn't part of her nature. She was a "pull-yourself-up-by-the-bootstraps-and-get-on-with-it" kind of gal. She didn't waste much energy feeling sorry for herself.

"I'm listening," Jack prompted.

Except for her two best girlfriends, nurse Lacy Calder and Dr. Janet Hunter, she'd never discussed the curse with anyone outside her family and she'd certainly never broached the subject with a man, but if anyone deserved an explanation it was Jack.

Besides, he wasn't like most guys. Jack was different—quiet, strong, understanding.

And therein lay the problem. Jack was a forever kind of guy, and CeeCee was *not* a forever kind of woman no matter how much she might wish she could be.

"Remember when I told you my mother had been married and divorced four times?" she asked.

Jack nodded. "So?"

CeeCee squirmed. "Even though I had four fathers, I had no real male role models."

"Don't tell me your mother's bad experiences have soured you on the entire institution of marriage. You're not your mother, CeeCee."

She raised a hand. "That's not the whole of it. It's a lot more complicated than that."

"Go on."

"I'm cursed."

A smile twitched at the corner of his lips. "Cursed?"

"My whole family is." Then in excruciating detail, she told the story of Grandma Addie and the fortuneteller.

When she had finished, Jack stared at her incredulously. "You're such a smart woman. I can't believe you would buy into that ridiculous myth."

"It's not ridiculous," she denied, feeling a tad defensive that he thought she should be able to overcome a lifetime of indoctrination by a sheer effort of will. He had no idea what it was like to live with the Jessup family whammy.

"Okay, it's a *dangerous* myth."

"It's not a myth. See this?" She fingered the charms on the gold bracelet adorning her left wrist.

"Yes. You're always wearing it."

"The bracelet's a reminder."

"Of what?"

"To stay single. Each charm represents the occupation of all seventeen of my family members' ex-husbands."

"You're kidding."

"Nope. There's dice for my gambling grandfather. He's the one who left the fortuneteller for Grandma Addie, but she went through two more husbands before finally calling it quits. The saxophone is for my father. Haven't seen him in fifteen years. Last I heard he was playing in strip clubs in New Orleans."

She held out her wrist and picked another charm to hold up to the light. "A race car for Aunt Sophia's seventh husband. A wine bottle for Aunt Beverly's alcoholic second mate. A tennis racket for my sister Geena's cheating soon-to-be first ex-husband."

"That's bizarre, CeeCee."

"Tell me about it."

"All right, I'll grant you it's not just a myth. It seems to be a self-fulfilling prophecy in your family. Somehow the fortuneteller scared your grandmother badly enough to believe in the evil eye. Your grandmother passed on her screwball values. Your mother and your aunts and you and your sister bought into them. Are you really going to allow your grandmother's fears to rule the rest of your life?"

"The fortuneteller vowed no male babies would be born into the Jessup family for three generations and guess what? None have been. How do you explain that, Mr. Skeptic?"

"Coincidence."

CeeCee shrugged. "Maybe. But I'm not taking any chances. I've seen enough divorce to last me two lifetimes. No need to make those same mistakes on my own."

"You wouldn't." Jack's brown eyes shone with certainty.

But CeeCee wasn't so sure.

"Self-fulfilling prophecy or not, the Jessup family whammy is no laughing matter. It's very real. And I don't have a clue what makes a loving relationship work. I made up my mind a long time ago. The curse dies with me. I'll never marry and have children."

Jack made a choking noise. "I'm not afraid of your curse."

"I am."

Setting his glass down on the coffee table, he leaned forward and took her hand in his. "Why don't you give me a chance to show you that you're wrong? Somewhere deep inside your heart you know exactly what it takes to love and be loved."

She shook her head.

"Go out with me, CeeCee. I know we would be great together."

"I can't," she whispered. She felt a drop of moisture on her cheek, and this time it wasn't water.

"Why not?" He tapped his foot, impatient, antsy. "Let me prove to you not all men are like your father and Lars. Let me show you I'm different."

"I can't jeopardize our friendship, Jack. I won't lose that."

He clenched his jaw and got to his feet. "You're turning me down?"

"Yes, but only for your own good."

"Friendship isn't enough for me anymore, CeeCee. I want you. I've wanted you from the first time I set eyes on you. I've helped you pick up the pieces every time one of those guys has dumped on you. I'm telling you I can't keep watching you hurt yourself."

CeeCee's eyes widened in alarm, and her chin trembled. "What are you saying, Jack?"

"I'm saying..." He paused a moment. "I don't think we can continue being friends."

3

"Something's wrong with Jack," CeeCee told her girlfriends, Lacy and Janet.

They were browsing a bridal shop in search of bridesmaids dresses they could agree on for Lacy's impending wedding.

"Wrong?" Janet raised an eyebrow. "How so?"

"He's acting really weird." CeeCee rubbed her chin. She'd been fretting about Jack all day.

"What about these?" asked Lacy, a petite blonde surgical nurse. She fingered pink, puffy-sleeved taffeta dresses with bustles.

"No!" CeeCee and Janet cried in unison.

"Come on," Lacy coaxed. "They'd go perfectly with the lime-green tuxes I've got picked out for the men."

Janet and CeeCee exchanged horrified glances.

34

"Wh-what?" CeeCee stammered.

Janet growled. "Forget it. I'm not dressing up like some bubblegum Southern belle and standing next to some guy who looks like a toxic spill,"

Janet, a tall, willowy brunette with indigo eyes, possessed a no-nonsense personality that counterbalanced Lacy's inherent sweetness and CeeCee's usual optimism and CeeCee loved her to pieces.

"Gotcha." Lacy laughed and pointed a finger at them. "I was kidding."

"Thank heavens," CeeCee said. "I thought we were going to have to call in the fashion police and have you carted away for violation of the good taste code."

"Go ahead." Lacy waved a hand. "I didn't mean to joke in the middle of your problem. What happened with Jack?"

"Last night he told me he could no longer be my friend." CeeCee pushed a hand through her curls.

"Seriously?" Janet scowled.

Jack's declaration caused a strange emptiness inside her chest, and CeeCee couldn't say why. As an outgoing, gregarious woman, she had tons of friends. Why would the loss of one guy affect her so strongly, especially when she was accustomed to losing the men in her life on a regular basis?

"What?" Lacy asked. "But why would he do that?

Bennett says Jack is about the nicest resident at St. Madeleine's."

"Jack is a great guy and he's a wonderful doctor. He interned with me last fall, remember," Janet agreed. "What did you do to him, Cee?"

"It's the curse," CeeCee whispered.

Always a bridesmaid, never a bride.

"Oh, please." Janet rolled her eyes. "Not that excuse again."

"It's bad enough the darned curse keeps me from ever getting married, but now it's even causing trouble in my friendship with Jack," CeeCee said.

"Hogwash." Janet shook her head impatiently. "There's no such thing as a curse."

"I don't know about that. If there's such a thing as the Thunderbolt," Lacy said, referring to the incredible love-at-first-sight zap that had caused her and Dr. Bennett Sheridan to fall head over heels in love. "Why can't CeeCee be a victim of the Jessup family whammy?"

"You're not helping," Janet told Lacy. "CeeCee us to bolster her confidence, not perpetuate her belief in some superstitious mumbo jumbo. C'mon you two. We're women of science. We should act like it."

CeeCee turned her back on her friends and blinked away the tears gathering in her eyes. They didn't understand. No one understood what it was like to grow up in a fractured household where the men came and went like taxicabs.

She had spent a lifetime trying to make lemonade from lemons, grinning and bearing it. Never getting too attached to any stepfather, step-uncle, step-grandfather.

For the most part she maintained an optimistic attitude. She didn't want to marry knowing it could only end in disaster, but she *did* want Jack's friendship. More than she'd ever realized until the threat of losing him loomed.

"Start from the beginning." Janet placed a hand on CeeCee's shoulder and guided her to a table and chairs situated in the back of the shop for customer convenience. "Now exactly what happened?"

"Jack asked me out."

"The beast!" teased Lacy.

"What a brute! You want us to call the law on him?" Janet joined in.

"Ha-ha."

"Come on, Cee, is it so tragic that he asked you out?" Janet looked puzzled.

CeeCee gazed at her dark-eyed friend. "Yes. I like him too much to hurt him."

"Do you suppose he could be in love with you?"

She froze. *Please, no, don't let it be so.*

"Of course not." CeeCee forced a laugh. Then she

remembered the kiss and the way Jack had touched her, the look on his face. Groaning, she closed her eyes.

"Do you want to be more than friends?" Janet nudged her.

"It's not an option, Janet. I can never fall in love. Ever. And especially not with Jack. He's the kindest, most gentle man I know, and I will not hurt him by getting romantically involved with him."

THREE DAYS HAD PASSED AND CeeCee WAS IN THE hospital swimming pool assisting a stroke victim with the woman's aquatic exercises when her assistant, Deirdre, came over and told her that Dr. Travis wanted to see her.

She glanced the door, spotting Jack standing in the archway.

He wore green hospital scrubs, white leather sneakers, and had a black stethoscope tossed around his neck. His hair was sexily mussed, as if he'd been repeatedly raking his fingers through it.

Her pulse hip hopped. She hadn't seen him since that fateful night, and she worried he was upset with her.

"Deirdre," she asked, surprised by the tremor in her voice. "Could you finish up with Mrs. Mathers?"

"Sure."

She and Deirdre switched places. CeeCee came up the ladder, fully aware Jack's eyes were on her. She reached for a towel, wrapped it around her waist, and slid her feet into a pair of flip-flops. Pasting a pleasant smile on her face, she sallied to the door.

"Hi!" She greeted him as if they'd never had an argument, as if everything was hunky-dory and she hadn't spent her nights tossing and turning and worrying that she had wounded his feelings by refusing to date him.

"Sorry to take you from your work."

"No problem. You want to go into my office?"

She indicated a door at the other end of the physical therapy room. A few patients ran on treadmills with monitors attached to their chests. Others lay on mats enduring range-of-motion exercises, or practiced crutch walking with attendants. Weights clanged. Voices echoed against the tall ceilings.

"We can talk here. It won't take long," he said.

Was he that afraid of being alone with her? CeeCee searched his face.

His expression was deadpan.

Anxiously she ran her tongue over her lips. All right, all right, she was the one afraid of being alone with him. She feared her hormones would kidnap her brain and do something really insane—like throw Jack on her desk and kiss him until he begged for mercy.

"Okay. What's up?" She forced a carefree note into her voice. No renegade estrogen was gonna boss her around.

His gaze flicked over her. His pupils widened. Self-consciously, she unfurled the towel from her waist and held it to her chest.

"I've come to say goodbye."

"Goodbye?" Her heart dived to her tummy.

Plunk!

He nodded solemnly.

"You're leaving St. Madeleine's?"

"Not forever."

"How long?"

"For the rest of the summer." The corners of his eyes softened, his smile deepened, and her tummy, which was currently swimming somewhere around her ankles, turned to pure mush. "Until September."

"B-but where are you going?" she asked, feeling strangely abandoned. It was a familiar sensation. She should be quite used to it by now.

Why Jack should be any different, she couldn't say, but her disappointment was as barbed as the day her real father had told her and her sister,

Geena that he was moving to Louisiana without them.

"I'm headed for Mexico. Remember, I told you I'd applied to volunteer for Dr. Blakemoore's surgical team?"

Yes, she recalled. He'd mentioned something about joining a group of doctors and nurses from St. Madeleine's who traveled to poverty-stricken countries every summer to provide free medical care to children in need. She even considered signing onto the project herself, but it hadn't fit with her work schedule.

Now, she wished she had made a way to go so she could be with him.

And that, right there, was a dangerous thought. She should be distancing herself from him, not getting closer. It looked like fate was doing the separating for her.

Good, good, she told herself, but it did not feel good at all.

"I was placed on the alternate list," he continued, "and at the last minute one of the surgeons had to drop out, so I got bumped up. Since my internship is over and my orthopedic residency doesn't start until September, this opportunity came at a great time. It even saves me from having to teach a lab class in summer school.

"Oh." CeeCee cleared her throat. "Well, that's great, I suppose."

"It's a great opportunity. I'll learn a lot."

It was terrific that he so willingly gave of himself to others, but on a selfish note, she was going to miss him something fierce.

He shifted his weight but held her gaze. "I also thought it might give us both some time to think things over."

She nodded. "Um-hmm."

"I brought you the key to my apartment." He passed the key over to her.

She clutched it in her palm. It was still warm from his body heat.

"If you don't mind, could you water my plants and feed my fish?"

"Of course."

"And here's the number to the place where we'll be staying, too." He took a slip of paper from his pocket and handed it to her. "This is where I'll be staying. Just in case you need to reach me for any reason. There are no cell phone service in the village we're going to so if I don't call back right away, don't worry."

"You go on to Mexico and don't fret about a thing here. Have a wonderful time. Help those children. Learn a lot."

"Thanks. I hope to."

He nodded, his gaze never leaving hers. He wanted to say more, she could see it in his eyes. But no words would soothe the bizarre sensation that he was leaving for good.

So what? the tiny voice in the back of her mind sniped. The defensive voice from her childhood that reared up whenever some man left. *Ta-ta. Bye-bye. So long chum. Been nice knowing ya. Don't let the door hit you on the way out. Who needs you anyway?*

"Is that it?" she asked.

"Oh, one other thing. My twin brother, Zack, might be dropping by to stay at my apartment while he's in town for a competition. He's the motocross champion, remember."

"Of course."

"Actually, you two will probably hit it off. He's mad for adventure. He even goes by the moniker Wild Man on the circuit."

"He sounds like you're opposite."

"He is. Zack loves extreme sports and never dates any one woman for too long. He's always on the move, looking for excitement. Your kind of guy."

CeeCee didn't know what to say. In a perfect world, Jack was *exactly* her type. But she couldn't have him. Although Zack did sound like a lot of fun but only because he would have no expectations of her.

No strings attached. How could she explain her fears to Jack so he could understand?

Besides, it would be weird getting involved with Jack's twin brother. She suppressed a shudder at that thought. Nope. No. Not going there.

"Did you hear me?" Jack asked.

"Are you identical twins?"

"In DNA, if not temperament. Yes."

Jack and Zack looked exactly alike? Then definitely not. She couldn't date her best guy friend's twin.

"Anyway, I percolated on your dilemma with the charity auction, after you lost Lars—"

"That was sweet of you, but I'll figure something out."

"Hopefully, you won't have to. I phoned Zack and asked if he could help out. Zack couldn't make any promises. He's not a promise-making kind of guy, but he said he'd try to be there for you event and I told him he could crash at my place."

"That's so sweet of you." His kindness touched her deeply and she almost threw her arms around him, but then the thought of what she might stir up held her back. All right, Jack was better than most.

He shrugged and gave her a lazy grin that lit up her spirits. "It was the least I could do after chasing off your pro-wrestler."

"You're so thoughtful." She laughed at his droll expression.

His eyes darkened and his smile disappeared. "Thoughtfulness hasn't gotten me anywhere with you."

"Oh, Jack." She reached out a hand and touched his cheek.

"I'm going to miss you, CeeCee."

"I'll miss you, too."

This was awful. Too bad Jack wasn't a self-centered, macho male who wanted nothing more than a casual fling. That, she could handle. Then again, if he were a self-centered, macho male she wouldn't worry about hurting him.

Despite her best intentions not to notice him in a sexual way, she found herself studying his strong profile, and admiring the way his short hair lay against his head.

He was a good-looking man. Perhaps it was a positive thing that he was leaving town. By the time he returned, she'd have her attraction to him firmly under control.

Jack cleared his throat and gestured toward the door. "I've got to go. I've barely got enough time to round up my gear before the van leaves for the airport."

"You're leaving right now?"

"Yes. May I ask another favor of you?"

"Of course, but I can't make any promises."

He smiled ruefully. "You sound just like Zack."

"What is it?" she murmured.

"Will you think about me, about us, while I'm gone?"

"Jack..."

"It's okay." He eyed her regretfully. "Your tone of voice just answered my question."

4

A month later, Jack rattled north across the Texas/Mexico border in the bed of a 1952 Ford pickup truck. He was being driven home because one, he couldn't afford the flight on his meager intern's salary and two, because it was almost as far from the little Mexican village that he'd been working in, to the nearest Mexican airport, as it was to drive straight to Houston.

His injured left knee, which he could barely bend, ached like the dickens, rivaling the chronic ache that had festered in his heart for four long weeks after he'd left CeeCee behind. She wasn't expect him home until September.

Jack took another slug off the tequila that Pedro, the pickup driver, had given him to ease his discomfort during the nine-hour journey home in the truck bed. He rode in the back because sitting in the cab of truck intensified the pain in his knee.

Another slug of hooch and Jack found himself tongue-to-tongue with the worm.

He'd reached rock bottom.

"*Ay-riba!*" he sang to the darkness and swallowed the worm whole.

If CeeCee Adams could see him now. Drunk, knee busted, eating tequila-soaked worms. Very Zack-like. He hadn't shaved or cut his hair the entire time he'd been out of the country. His skin was bronzed to the color of whole wheat toast by the relentless Mexican sun even though he'd used sunscreen.

Wild? CeeCee wanted wild? He'd show her wild.

Pedro slowed the truck as they approached the Houston city limits and stopped at a signal light. He stuck his head out the driver's side window. "You okay, amigo?"

"*Mucho fino*," Jack sang and wondered why the city lights kept fading in and out.

"You're going to have one helluva headache tomorrow."

"I know."

He needed some kind of crutch. He wasn't ready to see CeeCee again. He had planned on being away for eight weeks. In eight weeks he might have come up with a plan for winning her over. A plot to convince her that she wasn't cursed, that they could make a perfect couple and live happily ever after.

But four weeks simply wasn't long enough to form a dazzling plan. For the last month, he'd done nothing except work twelve-hour days and pine for CeeCee. When he wasn't in surgery or checking up on the kids in recovery, his mind had been on his best friend.

Correction. His ex-best friend.

Then he had dislocated his knee by stepping into a gopher hole while carrying an anesthetized child to the post-op tent. And bingo! The doctor heading their team had insisted he return to Houston for rest and physical therapy before starting his orthopedic residency. He was coming home four weeks early and completely unprepared for seeing CeeCee again.

"Is this the place?" Pedro asked.

Jack propped himself up on his elbow and peered over the bed of the pickup. He squinted at the entrance to his apartment complex and spied a mass of haphazardly parked cars.

Patio lanterns had been lit. Sounds of conversation, laughter, and splashing in the pool carried easily on the late-night air.

"Yeah."

"Sounds like a party," Pedro observed.

Jack knew who was throwing the party. It had to

be the same gregarious woman who instigated most of the River Run soirees.

CeeCee Adams.

Pedro parked, got out of the pickup, and came around to let the tailgate down. Jack ran a hand through five hundred miles of windblown hair, then scooted to the end of the truck bed.

"You want me to help you to your door before I go to my girlfriend's house?" Pedro asked. "She only lives a few miles from here."

"Nah." Jack gestured in the direction of the cars. "My friends are here. They'll help me."

"You sure?"

Jack nodded. The truth was he didn't want his friends and colleagues to see him limping through the complex, leaning on Pedro's shoulder. He had gone to Mexico to help children, not to wrench his knee and return a failure.

Pedro unloaded Jack's duffel bag. "I'll carry it for you."

"I can manage."

"Amigo, you can barely walk."

"Thanks, Pedro. I'll be fine." The slur in his voice denied his words.

Pedro shook his head. "You one proud dude, Dr. Travis."

Jack pulled a wad of bills from the pocket of his jeans and passed them to Pedro. "For gas money."

Pedro hesitated a moment, then took the cash. He clasped Jack on the shoulder. "I hope you win her," he said.

"Win who?"

"The *senorita* who has kept you so sad." Pedro flashed a smile, then hopped in his truck and drove away.

Even Pedro had seen through him. He wasn't ready to face CeeCee when his heart was still so obviously stuck to his sleeve.

Sighing, Jack shouldered his duffel bag and gingerly tested his knee.

Ow! Ouch! Okay. Bad idea.

Nine hours of sitting in the back of the truck hadn't improved his circulation or his range of motion. He glanced around. If he could hop to the fence, he could use it to brace himself up to the sidewalk from there, he could slip through the apartments, using the buildings themselves as support and keep to the shadows so he wouldn't be spotted by the partygoers.

Good plan except the tequila had affected his equilibrium.

He commanded his head to stop spinning. By

some miracle he made it to the fence and clung there a moment, struggling to get his balance.

He inched forward one painful step at a time.

At last, he came to the end of the fencing. From his vantage point, hidden in shadows, he could see the pool area.

Many of his colleagues from the hospital, decked out in swimwear, were there. Rock music filled the air along with the smell of barbecue and watermelon.

CeeCee was throwing an all-out wingding, something she often did when she needed a pick-me-up. When she felt blue, she didn't dress in sweats, hole up with sad movies, and guzzle gallons of Butter Brickle ice cream. She threw parties, and the bigger the better.

Was CeeCee depressed? Could she be longing for him the way he was longing for her? His heart leapfrogged at the possibility. Jack spotted CeeCee's friend, Lacy, sitting poolside kissing her fiancé, Dr. Bennett Sheridan. He recognized her other friend, Dr. Janet Hunter, serving drinks. He kept searching the crowd, and at last he found what he was looking for.

CeeCee.

Wearing the skimpiest aqua string bikini he'd ever seen. Her wet hair was slicked back off her face. She looked as fetching as a mermaid. With those honed curves, the woman could have posed for the cover of *Sports Illustrated*.

She was leaning over a lawn chair talking to some man he didn't know. The guy's gaze was welded to her cleavage. Obviously, she hadn't been pining away for him. He had misinterpreted the reason for her party.

What did you expect, nimrod?

Then a terrible thought occurred to him. What if the family curse story had just been an excuse to let him down easy?

The guy in the lawn chair moved closer to CeeCee and whispered something in her ear. She swatted friskily at him, then threw back her head and laughed.

Jack grit his teeth as jealousy turned to battery acid in his throat. Damn! He didn't need to see that. He gulped and turned his head away.

He had to get to his apartment. Before he did something really stupid like limp over to the pool and punch the guy's lights out. Palm splayed on the side of the building, he eased forward and stumbled over a hibachi. The thing clanged loudly.

"Shhh!" Jack cast a furtive glance back at the pool. No one noticed. Pushing the hibachi back in place with the toe of a charcoal-smeared sneaker, he struggled on.

He finally reached his apartment and dropped his

duffel on the front stoop, only to realize when he went to open the front door that he had given his only key to CeeCee. He would rather break into his own apartment than make show up in his current condition.

He managed to stay out of sight from the revelers while prying the screen off his window. Now came the hard part, smashing the glass without drawing attention.

"Pretty desperate, Travis," he muttered.

But he was desperate. He was also more than a little drunk, a lot jealous, and rather teed off at himself for not coming up with a better plan. Right now, however, he wanted nothing more than to collapse into the bed and sleep for twenty hours straight.

With that objective in mind, he peeled off his T-shirt, wrapped it around a fist, and gave the window-pane a quick, hard jab.

The glass fell inward onto his bedroom carpet with hardly a sound. Between the laughter, the splashing, and a raucous updated version of "Wild Thing," he was sure no one in the pool area heard him. Tomorrow, he'd replace the pane; tonight his body thirsted for sleep.

Slipping a hand through the hole he'd made, he fumbled for the latch. And felt something hard and cold press into his back. Something that felt suspiciously like the nose of a gun.

CeeCee's knees slammed together harder than loose shutters in a hurricane. When she had gone upstairs to fetch a fresh bucket of ice, she'd caught sight of someone trying to break into Jack's apartment.

Without thinking twice, she'd grabbed the flashlight from the kitchen drawer and ran downstairs to confront the prowler.

She hadn't stopped to think whether the intruder could be dangerous. She'd promised Jack she'd keep an eye on his place, and damn if she'd would allow a sneak thief to make off with his things while he was off saving lives.

Besides, half of St. Madeleine's doctors were swimming in the complex's pool. If she needed help, she could throw back her head and scream bloody murder.

"Hold it right there, buster," she growled, pressing the butt of the flashlight into his bare back in hopes he'd believe she had a gun. "Put your hands over your head."

"And if I refuse?"

CeeCee gulped. She hadn't counted on that. "I'll pull the trigger and blow you to kingdom come."

"I'd pay to see that trick," he drawled. "Since I've never heard of anyone getting shot by a flashlight."

The voice sounded familiar. Very familiar.

"Jack?"

Slowly, the man turned, and CeeCee found herself staring into Jack's deep-brown eyes. Except nothing else about the guy felt familiar. He smelled of tequila, and Jack only drank beer, and rarely that. His hair was long, his beard scraggly. His bare, muscled chest was darkly tanned, and he was favoring his left knee. The guy might look like Jack, but he was five pounds leaner and had a thrilling lawless quality about him.

The air of a very bad boy inviting her to a bedroom romp.

The quality stirred an instant response in her. Their gazes locked and CeeCee found it hard to catch her breath.

Her pulse bounced like busted bedsprings—*boing, boing, boing.* In that moment she realized what she'd found.

One hot, sexy, motocross champion.

CeeCee dropped the flashlight to her side and grinned. "Hey, everyone," she shouted, waving to the crowd below. "Come on over and meet Jack's identical twin brother, Zack."

JACK HAD NEVER INTENDED ON LYING TO CEECEE. She'd simply assumed he was Zack, and before he could correct her, she'd tucked his arm in hers and leaned her lithe body against his bare chest.

Her breast swayed delicately against his nipple. Her skin was velvet on his. She smelled of coconuts and pineapples and sheer blue heaven.

A cold sweat popped out on his forehead. Suddenly, despite the tequila he'd consumed, Jack was stone-cold sober.

"Hi, Zack," she whispered in a sweet, sexy voice he'd never heard her use. A delightful voice that raised goose bumps on his arms and sent a shaft of pure desire arrowing straight to his groin. "You're here way early for the charity auction."

"Uh-huh." Overwhelmed by his reaction, he barely mustered the sound.

CeeCee had never looked more beautiful. With that passion-red hair curling around her shoulders, her full lips tinted with a whisper of pink lip gloss, her damp swimsuit clinging to every curve, she resembled an ethereal water nymph.

Mythical, magical, enchanting.

Jack stared as if seeing her for the first time.

Through Zack's fresh eyes. He even heard his brother's voice rumble through his head.

Whew-ee, bro, she's the bomb! Long legs. Perky breasts. Hair like liquid fire. Cheeky dimples. You've got yourself a sizzling-hot, stone-cold fox.

Except CeeCee wasn't his.

And she was so much more than a "fox." She was fun and smart, a delight to be around. She cried at sad movies and threw pennies in wishing wells. She smiled often and rarely held a grudge. She cared about others and gave unselfishly of herself. She had legions of friends and not a single enemy that he knew of.

Well, maybe except for Lars Vandergrin, but who cared about him?

CeeCee was perfection walking.

And he wanted her desperately. Not just for now. Not for a night. Not for a four-week affair, but for a lifetime.

"I'm CeeCee." She flashed him a winsome dimple. "It's wonderful to meet you at last. Your brother has told me so much about you."

Jack gulped, uncertain what to do next. He opened his mouth to tell her the truth, but then without warning, he caught himself replying in a voice as provocative as CeeCee's own, "All bad, I trust."

Where the hell had that come from?

She giggled. "Jack warned me you were an outrageous flirt."

"That's me, outrageous."

"Hey, Zack!"

The crowd from the pool had moved their way. Dr. Bennett Sheridan thrust out a hand in greeting. Bennett had been the resident overseeing Jack's internship during his rotation through cardiac surgery earlier in the year. Bennett had his other arm draped around Lacy's waist. "Great to meet you, buddy. Jack speaks of you often."

Awkwardly, Jack shook Bennett's hand. Shame had him avoiding his mentor's gaze. Other party guests, most of them people he knew from the hospital or the apartment complex, welcomed him, too, increasing Jack's uneasiness. CeeCee's mistake sewed him up. How could he get out of this without embarrassing them both?

"Let's go sit by the pool," CeeCee said.

He held back, feeling exposed walking around in nothing but his blue jeans, his bare chest on display.

"My shirt." He gestured toward the shattered windowpane. "I used it to break the glass. I er...forgot that Jack said you had his key."

"Don't worry about going shirtless. It's a pool party. No one cares what you wear. We've got food and drink and a wide selection of music. Let me guess, I bet you're an indie rock fan."

Silently, Jack nodded. He didn't care for indie rock, but Zack did.

"Janet," CeeCee hollered and waved at her friend across the courtyard who was manning the stereo system. "Put on Artic Monkeys."

Janet complied and "Do I Wanna Know?" beat from the outdoor speakers placed strategically around the pool area, and the song expressed Jack's sentiments exactly. He wanted CeeCee to never stop hanging on to him, never stop gazing his way with adoring eyes.

"And I bet you could go for a margarita on the rocks, right?" CeeCee beamed at him, her fingers wrapped possessively around his upper arm.

Actually, he was thirsty for a tall drink of CeeCee and the last thing he needed was more tequila clouding his brain, making him do dumb things like keep pretending he was his twin brother.

Speaking of which, this masquerade wasn't right. He should come clean before things really got out of hand.

But excitement showed in every feature on CeeCee's delicate face and she was chattering so fast he could hardly make out what she was saying. He thought she might be lauding his motocross skills.

Apparently, she was quite thrilled to meet Zack.

Jealousy, the green-eyed beast, charged through him like an ambulance dispatched to the scene of a serious accident. Simultaneously, his gut clenched in disappointment. As himself, he had never induced this kind of enthusiasm in CeeCee.

"Jack tells me you're footloose and fancy-free." She sent him a coquettish, sidelong glance. "A no-strings-attached kind of guy."

As opposed to Jack, a forever kind of man. The kind of man that CeeCee's ridiculous family curse wouldn't allow her to date.

And then it hit him. A bolt from the blue.

The answer to his problem with CeeCee. He'd been cast so deeply into "friend zoned" that CeeCee had stopped seeing him a viable sexual partner and the only way out of the zone was to change her entire perception of him.

Owza.

Why *not* become Zack? He wasn't due at the hospital for another month. Everyone thought he was still in Mexico.

Here, dropped right into his lap, was a primo opportunity to prove to CeeCee she could fall in love with a good, steady guy. Even if he had to use his brother's persona to convince her. He might not be as interesting as his twin, but dammit, curse or no friggin' curse, he knew in his soul he and CeeCee were meant to be together. If the only way she would give him a chance was as a sexy motorcycle champion, then he would become that man. Anything to win her.

"Yeah." Jack grinned wolfishly, playing his part to the hilt. "That's me. The happy wanderer. Never in one place for too long. Fathers have been known to lock up their daughters when I roll into town."

"You're scandalous." Grinning, she swatted him lightly on the shoulder, causing his blood to pump like a faucet.

"Don't ever forget it, sweetheart." He forced himself to remain nonchalant. In actuality, he was about to split right out of his skin.

She was so close and smelled so nice.

He was acutely aware of her long bare limbs and her lovely cleavage threatening to overflow her skimpy bikini top. In fact, Jack realized too late, he was drilling a hole through her with his stare.

She blushed and ducked her head.

Jack marveled. He'd managed to fluster the unflappable CeeCee. Amazing.

"Let's pour you a drink." She took his hand and led him toward the makeshift bar set up near the diving board.

He walked gingerly beside her.

"Hey." She stopped and peered at his leg. "You're limping."

"Don't worry. It's nothing."

"What happened?" Her eyes widened to the size of quarters. "A motorcycle crash?"

That certainly sounded more macho than the truth, but he was still uncomfortable out-and-out lying to her, so he simply nodded.

"*Oooh*," she said, clearly impressed with his supposed recklessness. "Was the crash scary?"

He shrugged, doing the strong, silent number.

"Does it hurt?"

"A little." That was true.

"Poor baby," she murmured, her tone filled with compassion.

He was torn, part of him wanted to act tough; another part of him wanted to milk her sympathy for all it was worth.

What would Zack do?

Zack wouldn't be standing here gaping at her like some tongue-tied simpleton. Zack would take full advantage of the situation. Somehow, Zack would have her in his apartment giving him a rubdown in five minutes flat.

A shudder knifed through Jack at the thought of CeeCee's fingers gliding over his skin.

"Well..." He lowered his head until his cheek was

almost touching hers. "If you promise not to tell anyone, my knee is aching a lot. I've been traveling all day, and I'm ready for bed."

At least that was the truth.

"Oh my goodness, I'll bet it is. You must be exhausted. And here I've been yammering my head off." She took a step away from him, and he noticed her chest was rising and falling in a quick, heady rhythm, unexpectedly matching his own. "Did Jack tell you I'm a physical therapist?"

"He mentioned it."

She nodded, her fiery-red curls bouncing. "I could look at your knee if you like. Maybe massage it for you."

If he liked?

Not to seem overeager and frighten her away, Jack barely lifted one shoulder. "I don't want to take you away from your party."

She waved a hand. "Never mind. The party'll be breaking up soon. Most people have to work tomorrow and anyway my friends Janet and Lacy are sharing the hostess duties."

"Well...if you're sure. A massage does sound great." His ease at lying both surprised and shamed him.

"You wait right here," CeeCee said. "I'll locate Jack's key in my apartment and let you in properly.

Then we'll tuck you into bed and massage your leg. And in the morning, we'll tell the superintendent the windowpane needs replacing."

Tuck him into bed? Hot damn.

"That's really sweet of you, CeeCee."

"Hey, Jack's my best friend in the whole world. I would do anything for him. And that includes taking care of his twin brother."

And I'd do anything in the world for you, CeeCee. Anything at all. Even pretend to be my own twin.

"I won't be a second." She touched him briefly on the arm, then took off upstairs.

His eyes followed her graceful movements. His stomach hitched a ride to his throat. She was captivating, stunning, absolutely breathtaking. If he played his cards right, before this month was out, he'd be out of the friend zone and into her bed.

And Dr. Jack Travis wanted nothing more in the entire world.

🦂 5 🦂

CeeCee's hands trembled as she fumbled in her junk drawer for the key to Jack's apartment.

Was Zack destined to become a scorching affair? In other words, Jack antivenom so she could stop fixating on her best friend.

"Calm down," she chided after she dropped the key for the third time on her way out the front door. "Chill. You're getting ahead of yourself."

Understatement of the year.

Fifteen minutes with Zack and already her libido wanted to stampede right off a cliff. For the first time since Jack left, CeeCee realized how much her midnight sexual fantasies had taken their toll.

Was she so gosh-darned hungry for her best friend she was willing to vault into the sack with his look-alike twin to sate her appetite? It was a natural urge, but to act on those urges wouldn't be fair to either Zack or Jack.

Or for that matter, her.

"Look what you've done to me, Jack Travis," she muttered under her breath. "And all I ever did was give you one little kiss on those killer lips. You've turned me into a nutcase. Thank heavens things never went any further between us."

She slipped out the door, key clutched firmly in her hand, and found Zack sprawled in a lounge chair surrounded by a throng of women.

Giggling, cooing, beautiful women draped over him like tablecloths. One sat in his lap. Two others leaned on each shoulder.

Hmph.

She'd run slap-dab against the downside of setting one's sights on a sexy rogue—fierce competition. But a little rivalry was fine with her. She wasn't looking for a forever kind of guy and she wasn't jealous. Zack was a charming free bird, and that's what she liked about him. No strings tying down this twin.

CeeCee approached the group, dangling the key at Zack. She wriggled her toes—painted Pretty-In-Pink just for the party—inside her strappy gold sandals and forced a casual smile.

"Ready, Romeo?" She couldn't resist.

Zack studied her toes, a contented expression on his face. She could have sworn he murmured something like, "And this little piggy cried wee-wee-wee all the way over to Zack's place."

What an ego.

"Zack," she said sternly.

"Yes, ma'am?" He raised his gaze and gave her a lazy wink.

Oh, but he was a player!

"Your knee. The pain. You wanted to lie down. Remember?"

Momentary irritation flashed through her. He was bold enough to flirt with her while three other women flanked him. She almost told him he could sweet-talk one of his new conquests into massaging his leg, but why let his behavior perturb her? It wasn't as if she cared. It wasn't as if he were his brother.

"Oh, yeah."

Grinning, he gently lifted the blushing young lady from his lap and cautiously rose to his feet. He tried to disguise his discomfort in his knee, but CeeCee detected his brief wince of pain and immediately her irritation vanished.

He was her best friend's brother. He'd been hurt. She was a physical therapist. She'd give him that massage.

It didn't have to mean anything.

"Nice meeting you, ladies," Zack said to his admirers.

The women tittered and grinned.

"This way, Lothario." CeeCee ushered him back across the courtyard toward Jack's apartment.

"Hey," he said. "I'm not as bad as all that."

"That's not what Jack tells me."

"My brother has a tendency to exaggerate."

CeeCee tossed a glance over her shoulder at the women who were still giggling and waving at Zack. "Oh, no? Then how do you explain *them*?"

"Jealous?" He chuckled.

"Of those women? Because of you? Get over yourself." CeeCee stopped on Jack's stoop and eyed Zack up and down before jamming the key into the lock with more force than she'd intended.

"CeeCee?"

"What?" she snapped and turned to find him standing right beside her.

His eyes glimmered darkly, from tequila or lust, she couldn't be sure which, maybe both. "Not one of those women can hold a candle to you."

For a brief second there, he sounded just like Jack. CeeCee caught her breath, then quickly expelled it. "Flatterer."

"I mean it."

"Yeah, right, Casanova." She wagged a finger under his nose. "You don't fool me."

"I've had my share of women." His breath was warm against her nape. "Does that bother you?"

"Why should your sexual history bother me?"

He quirked a smile, then reached out and traced a finger along her collarbone. "Because I was hoping..."

She knew what he was hoping. CeeCee turned away lightning quick before he spoke the words already on her mind. She nudged the door open.

"Ta-da," she exclaimed far too brightly as she flicked on the light and scurried inside.

He ambled in behind her, pulling the duffel bag that had been resting on the porch after him.

"Hey, that looks exactly like Jack's duffel."

"Does it?" With one foot, he nudged the bag behind him.

"I saw a program on one of those news shows about identical twins," she chattered, anxious to fill the air with sound. Anything to lessen the reality that she was wearing nothing but a string bikini and standing beside one of the most sexually potent men she'd ever run across.

"Apparently these two identical twins were separated at birth," she continued, "and didn't meet until they were in their thirties. Their similarities were uncanny."

70

"No kidding." He looked distracted, as if he was worried about something.

"They both had wives with the same name, and they drove the same make of car. They were both lawyers, and they liked the same foods."

"No kidding." He couldn't seem to take his eyes off her. It was disconcerting and rewarding, so she just kept blathering. "And when they bought each other a birthday gift for the first time, they gave the exact same shirt! Spooky, huh?"

"Spooky," he echoed.

"Is that how it is between you and Jack? You know, like telepathy?"

"Well..."

"Obviously, that must be the case to some degree. I mean you've both got the exact same duffel." She gestured at the bag again. "Just like those twins and their shirts." She was rattling on endlessly and she knew it, but she couldn't seem to stop.

"Jack and I really aren't that close. Despite being identical twins, we don't have much in common."

"Except for the duffel bag, of course."

"Oh, yeah, well that."

They stared at each other a long moment.

"Why don't you...um...head into the bedroom and shimmy out of those jeans?" she suggested.

"Why, CeeCee, that's the best offer I've had in weeks," he teased.

"You know what I mean." She mentally cursed her peaches-and-cream complexion that blushed so easily when she was befuddled.

"I'm sorry." He touched her shoulder. "I didn't mean to embarrass you."

"I'm not embarrassed," she denied although she felt her face heat to the flaming crimson of American Beauty roses. Zack was an odd guy. One minute, teasing and outrageous, the next almost like Jack, thoughtful and apologetic.

Zack telegraphed her a knowing grin, dispelling the notion he was the least bit like his twin brother.

She ducked her head, avoiding his eyes, and opened the door to Jack's bedroom. Glass lay on the carpet beneath the window. A breeze blew through the hole, lifting the curtain and bringing in sounds from the party.

"Holler when you're out of those pants and ready for the massage."

Zack sauntered into the room. CeeCee closed the door behind him, sagged against it on the other side, and waved a hand to fan herself. *Whew, somebody flip the air conditioning to arctic blast.*

A minute passed.

"CeeCee," Zack called.

"You ready?"

"Well...I'm having a problem."

She opened the door again and found him gazing sheepishly at her from the middle of the room. His jeans were unzipped, his rippling muscled chest still bare.

The sight was enough to make her eyes bug.

In the glow of the bedroom light he was thunderously breath-stealing. His tousled, collar-length hair and the beard covering his lean jaw gave him a knavish appearance. His skin was a burnished bronze, his grin devastating.

How had she ever thought this undisciplined man was anything like his kind, gentle twin? Jack and Zack were as different as dusk and dawn. One heralded the coming of darkness, the other celebrated daylight.

As much as she might long to reside in the daylight, it was her fate to spend her life in the dark thrill of night. Best to embrace destiny, not fight it.

"I couldn't shuck my jeans past my knee," Zack explained. "It's too swollen. I need you."

"Oh." CeeCee wet her lips with the tip of her tongue.

He wriggled his pants down over his hips, giving her full view of his white cotton briefs, and sat on the edge of the bed. CeeCee stayed rooted to the spot, staring, mouth agape.

"Come here." He crooked a finger at her.

No way. Uh-uh. She wasn't moving.

"CeeCee." His voice poured over her like warm brandy. "I *need* you."

How many times over the past four weeks had she imagined a scenario like this? Except in her fantasies it had been Jack on the bed calling her name—not his reprobate twin. But since she couldn't have the man she wanted, could Zack be the next best thing?

She was physically attracted to Zack, yes, siree, but only because he reminded her so much of Jack.

She was confused. She had an overwhelming desire to kiss Zack, to see if he tasted like Jack. A good sign or a bad one? Was she trying to sublimate her feelings for Jack by taking up with his brother?

A dangerous, wicked, forbidden thrill electrified her.

Being with Zack would be like having her cake and eating it, too. She wouldn't have to fear breaking gadabout Zack's heart. And he was exactly what she needed at the moment. Sexual anesthesia to take her mind off Jack.

Clearing her throat, she squared her shoulders and stepped across the room toward him.

He sat on the edge of the bed, slipped the jeans down over his good right leg, and extended his other leg toward her.

CeeCee knelt before him, her heart thudding so hard she feared it would explode in her chest. *Boom.* Grasping the denim material in both hands, she slowly began to work it over his swollen knee.

Winnowing his Levi's from around his ankle, she let the jeans drop to the floor, then slid her hands up his leg. Her fingers skimmed his honed calf muscles, tangled in the woolly hair on his shins, then came to rest on his knee. Gently she began to stroke him with soft, circular movements.

Zack hissed in his breath.

"Sore?"

"Uh-huh."

"Try and relax. You're very tense."

His laugh was hoarse. "Who wouldn't be tense with a fine-looking woman like you rubbing his knee?"

"You need to spend twenty minutes a day in the whirlpool, for two to three weeks," she said briskly, ashamed to admit his compliment pleased her.

CeeCee was accustomed to men making passes at her. She fended off pickup lines daily. Zack's desire for her was nothing new. What was new was her corresponding passion.

"Yeah, that's what the doctor told me. But I don't have access to a whirlpool."

"Yes, you do." She still avoided his gaze. Avoided

acknowledging that he was almost buck naked, that she was on her knees in front of him, that his nearness set her skin on fire. "We've got a whirlpool right here at the apartment complex, and I could give you a treatment every evening when I get home from work."

"Wow, that'd be great."

She finally caught his eye, beheld raw desire shimmering in the depths. He inhaled in rapid succession.

A fine sheen of perspiration glimmered off his one hundred percent fat-free chest. He possessed a devilishly sort of magic she couldn't ignore.

Trickery, witchery. I need help, she thought. A talisman, a good luck charm, something, anything to ward off his dangerous allure.

Oh! She pressed her teeth into her bottom lip to draw her focus to the task at hand and away from Zack's amazing body.

Did Jack look the same underneath his clothes? They were identical twins. The thought sent shivers capering up her spine like kids playing hopscotch.

"Stop doing that," he said hoarsely, causing CeeCee to lift her head and meet his gaze full-on.

"Am I hurting you?" Alarmed, she let go of his leg and rocked back on her heels.

"Yeah, but not in the way you think."

"Excuse me?" Puzzled, she cocked her head.

"Stop biting your bottom lip. It's driving me crazy."

"Huh?"

"Seeing those pearly teeth sinking into that full, lush bottom lip of yours makes me so..." His strangled voice trailed off, and then he whispered, "Hot."

He reached out and ran his thumb along the bottom lip in question. A lip tingling with electrical impulses. "It makes me want to kiss you."

She groaned softly. "Stop it, Zack."

"Why?" he asked. "It's obvious there's a powerful chemistry between us. Why ignore it, sweetheart?"

Then, before she could hightail it out of there, Zack hooked one arm around her waist, hauled her onto the bed with him, lowered his head, and kissed her.

❧ 6 ❧

Drunk on Zack's identity, the vestiges of cheap tequila, and the proximity of CeeCee's perfect little body—*abracadabra!* —Dr. Jack Travis was a man transformed.

She wore a string bikini. He was in his BVDs. Her dewy skin rubbed against his tanned hide. Her warm breath fanned the hairs on his forehead.

A sure recipe for disaster.

But Jack didn't care. He was no longer cautious, practical Dr. Travis. He was Wild Man Zack.

The desires he'd repressed for six months gushed like a geyser spewing hot energy into his system. The proverbial Jack had been sprung from his box.

Pop goes the weasel.

He ate her up, plunging heart and soul into that kiss.

His mouth absorbed her flavor. His tongue explored every corner of her warm, willing mouth. He kept his eyes wide open so he could see her, marveling at her long feathery lashes, the sweet curve of her cheek, and the way one bottom front tooth was just the slightest bit crooked. He was completely awed to have her in his bed.

He could scarcely believe she was here. He kept running his palms over the planes of her face to prove to himself she was real, and he wasn't caught up in a lucid dream.

Mine, he thought greedily. *Mine.*

In that moment he knew he had made the right decision by assuming his twin's persona. Anything, whatever it took to win her, was worth it.

CeeCee wriggled beneath him, mewling low in her throat.

Her feminine timbre, her dainty movements thrust him headlong into full-blown arousal. Passion gripped him and refused to let go. He was hard enough to punch holes in tin metal.

His blood surged through his veins, thundering in his ears louder than the ocean's surf. His temperature spiked as hot as Arizona in August. A whole blasted chorus of butterflies cavorted in his stomach, kicking like Vegas showgirls.

He reveled in her.

LORI WILDE

Silky lips. Satiny hair. Velvety fingertips. Downy nape.

Fuzzy. Fluffy. Plush and cuddly.

She was sweeter than the most heavenly dessert. Death by Chocolate, hell. Give him Death by CeeCee. What a way to go!

Down, down, down he fell into everything that was CeeCee. Her taste, her smell, her exquisite sounds. He couldn't stop his descent.

As if he wanted to!

For the first time in his life, he felt utter bliss. He closed his eyes, savoring the experience.

The moment lasted a good thirty seconds.

Then he screwed it up by saying, "I want you, CeeCee."

"Zack," CeeCee murmured, her mouth pressed to his, her small hands knotted into fists against his chest.

"Uh-huh." He drifted languidly in the pleasure, enjoying the way her whisper tickled his lips.

"We can't do this."

"Do what, babe?"

"Have sex."

Have sex? He wasn't having sex; he was making love.

No wait. Jack made love. Zack had sex and CeeCee thought he was Zack.

He couldn't let her think he wanted to make love instead of simply having wild circus sex. If she had the slightest inkling that he was crazy for her—as either Jack or Zack—she would dash away faster than the Roadrunner zipping off from Wile E. Coyote.

Beep. Beep.

Nonchalant, carefree, tons of fish in the sea, that was the attitude.

Yeah, easy to say. Now if only he could convince his heart to stop reeling into his rib cage every time that he looked at her.

He pried open his eyes. "I'm on fire for you, and I think you're hot for me, too. We're both consenting adults. What's the problem? Is it because I'm not interested in long-term?"

"Oh, no." She struggled to sit up.

He moved aside and watched her prop herself against the headboard and give him a look that was part regret, part longing. "No?"

"It's not that. I'm not interested in a long-term relationship, either. In fact, I never plan on marrying."

"Why not? Beautiful woman like you?" He reached out to finger a curl. He asked because he wanted to know if she'd tell Zack the same fantastic tale that she'd told him.

"It's a family curse." She waved a hand. "But I

don't want to get into it right now. Suffice it to say that because of my childhood, I don't believe in the institution of marriage."

"That's great, 'cause neither do I. Not that I had a bad childhood. In fact, my family was a bit like *Leave it to Beaver.* But heck, maybe that's why I want something different."

A thrill blasted through him. Yea! She hadn't made up that Jessup family whammy story simply to let Jack down easy.

"But," he continued, "I do believe in having a good time." It was hard knowing how to strike the right balance between Jack and Zack. He didn't want to come off egotistical, but on the other hand, he didn't want her to think he cared too much. Insouciance was the only thing that would keep her interested. "So let the good times roll."

"No. Not tonight. We've both been drinking and after all, we just met." Her curls bobbed seductively across the top of her breast. "Don't rush the thrill of the chase."

He had to glance at the ceiling for a second and compose himself, before turning his gaze back to those mesmerizing sea-green eyes.

"You're right." He took her hand and ran his thumb across her palm. "And I apologize if I overstepped my boundaries, but you're so damned sexy,

CeeCee; it's all I can do to keep my hands to myself."

"This isn't a forever no." She slanted him a coy, sideways glance that was almost his undoing. "Just a not-right-now no."

"So there's hope?"

She simply giggled.

"I pray that's a yes."

"I better go." She scooted off the bed. "My party guests are probably wondering where I've gotten off to."

Quick, do something, she's getting away.

"Are we still on for whirlpool treatments?" Jack gingerly rubbed his knee and sent her a hangdog expression, playing on her sympathy.

"Of course I'll still give you therapy. I'll see you Monday afternoon when I get off work."

"What about tomorrow?" he said. "On your day off."

"You're pretty persistent, aren't you?" She adjusted her swimsuit strap and smoothed down her mussed hair.

He angled her a grin. "Didn't Jack tell you? That's my middle name. Zack Persistent Travis."

"Until after you get a woman into bed, and then I bet your middle name switches to Zack See-Ya-Around Travis."

LORI WILDE

He laughed. "You've got my number."

She shook her head and chuckled. "That's what I like about you. You might be an intractable rapscallion, but at least you're honest about it."

"Rapscallion?" His laugh echoed hers.

"A bad boy."

"Babe," he drawled. "I'm no boy."

"Hmm." She raked her gave over him and licked her lips.

"CeeCee, I don't leave a trail of broken hearts behind me. I tell it like it is. Only those with heavily armored chest protectors need apply."

She leaned over, giving him a superior view of her excellent cleavage, and boldly chucked a finger under his chin.

Jack just about swallowed his tongue.

"You don't have to worry about me. After my crazy childhood, I've developed a heart of titanium. You'll never burn through it."

"Good," he said, but what he thought was *we'll see about that.*

"Until tomorrow." She turned away, wriggling her fingers behind her.

Until tomorrow, my sweet, he thought and watched her walk out the door.

Tonight, he'd struck out. But that was okay. He

had a whole month to convince her. Eventually he'd get her where he wanted her—denying that damned family curse and letting herself be loved.

Now all he had to do was find out how to burn a hole through titanium.

"So?"

CeeCee blinked at Janet. She'd been daydreaming about kissing Zack. Remembering how his lips had felt on hers—strong and hungry. Thinking that he tasted exactly like Jack. But of course, they were identical twins. And if it weren't for the scratchy beard, she could almost pretend he *was* Jack.

"So?" Janet repeated.

Focus. Here. Now. Get out of Zack's bedroom. "So, what?"

It was well after midnight, and the guests had departed. They were cleaning up the courtyard, stuffing plastic cups, aluminum cans, and paper plates into different colored trash bags for recycling.

"So, how was Jack's brother?"

"What do you mean how *was* he?"

"Come on, you were with him in Jack's apartment for almost an hour. Are you going to tell me your physical therapy session didn't turn a little more physical than a simple knee massage?"

"Janet! Why on earth would you even suggest such a thing?"

"You mean besides the hickey on your neck?"

"What!" Appalled, CeeCee slapped a hand to her throat.

"The other side," Janet pointed out.

"Oh gosh." She slumped into a nearby lawn chair. "Now everyone will know."

"CeeCee, you would have to be deaf, dumb, and blind not to see the sexual chemistry snapping between the two of you. The air was practically electric."

Groaning, CeeCee plunked her head in her hands. "I don't want Jack to find out about this. It would break his heart to know that I made out with his twin brother."

"Hmm. Made out? Just how far did you go?"

"Janet!" CeeCee lifted her head. "What do you think I am?"

"I think you're a healthy, red-blooded American woman with no strings tying her down, who came across a man who really turned her on."

"We just kissed."

"That's it?" Janet sounded disappointed. She sat at

the edge of the pool and dipped her toes into the water.

"Well, I was in my bikini and he was in his underwear so of course there was body-to-body contact. Is that second base?"

"Any touching below the waist?"

"No."

Janet stuck her hand out straight, twisted it in a half wave. "First base, stealing for second."

"Am I horrible?"

"Not at all, honey." Janet leaned over and shook her foot. "You're wonderful."

"I bet Jack wouldn't think so if he knew."

"Why are you so worried about Jack? He's over six hundred miles away and he never put a ring on it." Janet stared at CeeCee's bare hand.

"He probably would if I gave him half a chance. Hence the problem. I feel like I'm cheating on Jack. Sounds weird, doesn't it?"

"Considering that you're nothing more than friends, yes."

"I know. But I'm wondering if I'm simply attracted to Zack *because* he reminds me of Jack."

"Could be."

Why couldn't she shake this feeling she was betraying Jack? And why, the entire time she'd been kissing Zack, had she kept wishing that he was his twin brother?

"You're thinking too much," Janet said. "Where's the lighthearted, carefree CeeCee we know and love? I'm supposed to be the gloomy cynic in the bunch, remember?"

CeeCee smiled. Thank heavens for her friend's clarity. She was obsessing over nothing. "You're right. There's not a problem. I'm making a mountain out of a molehill. Jack is my friend. Zack is my patient. Neither one of them is my lover, and that's the way it's going to stay."

OKAY, THIS WAS THE PLAN. JACK HAD TO FIND A way to convince CeeCee to become Zack's lover. Or rather *his* lover. Doggone it, he was confusing himself with this identity shifting. It was getting so he didn't know where he ended, and Zack began.

Last night, in his delight at having discovered a surefire plan to help CeeCee overcome her fear of that silly family curse, he'd moved too quickly, scaring her with his boldness. Subtlety was the key. A slow, simmering seduction.

He would use Zack's persona to get her into bed, but it would be he, Jack, who would keep her there.

Once CeeCee realized that she could indeed fall in love, that she was worthy of all the love in the world.

That was his only goal. To give her the love she deserved, the life she secretly craved but was so afraid to reach for.

He had gotten the masquerade off to a good start. He had awoken just before noon with his first hangover ever. Head throbbing, he had stumbled to the medicine cabinet for three aspirins. After washing back the pills with a gallon of water, he checked his phone and noticed he'd gotten a voice mail from her.

Heart suddenly racing, he played it.

The second he heard CeeCee's voice spinning into his room, he forgot his aching temples. She was going out to lunch with her friends, but she could supervise his whirlpool treatment at three-thirty. Would that be all right?

Yes, he texted her. Three-thirty is perfect.

Spurred into action, he spent the next hour at the outdoor mall shopping for "Zack" clothes. Black leather pants, a leopard print Speedo, Harley-Davidson T-shirts. Although his beard was driving him crazy, he would not shave it, for he feared once the hair was gone the line between him and his twin would disappear. He needed the hair as a crutch to separate himself from his brother.

At least in his own mind.

Because the landlord had called and said he couldn't repair the window for two days and because he was bored with nothing else to do, he detoured by the hardware store for a new pane of glass and repaired the window in record time. Still it was only two o'clock.

He called Zack's house to tell him not to bother coming to the charity auction, that he'd act as his stand-in, but he got Zack's roommate who told him Zack was on a three-week motocross run. Had his twin forgotten his promise?

Jack made a mental note to call his brother again in three weeks. He didn't trust the roommate's message-relaying skills. He certainly couldn't have his twin showing up at an inopportune time and blowing his whole cover.

He spent the remaining time pacing his apartment and practicing his twin's lower-pitched, slower-paced speech patterns.

Every time he heard a car engine, he popped over to the living room window, lift the curtain, and study the parking lot, hoping to catch a glimpse of CeeCee returning home.

After about the nine hundredth time of peeking from behind the curtain, her lime-green late-model VW Bug slid into her parking space.

Stomach in his throat, Jack watched her get out

and toss her fiery mane over her shoulder in a familiar way that made his gut clutch.

She flowed up the stairs to her apartment, moving so gracefully it seemed her feet never touched the ground. She had on a lavender floral print dress with a matching beaded choker and cute little white ballet slippers.

Jack, realizing he'd been holding his breath, inhaled deeply, his gaze fixed on her trim athlete's hips. The door closed behind her, and he moved away from the window, perspiration beading his forehead.

She gives me a fever, he thought, delirious with need. Break out the aspirin STAT! Grab an ice pack or two. And while you're at it, wheel in a defibrillator in case my heart stops.

His cell phone rang.

Jack shot across the room and snagged it off the table where he'd left it. "'Lo" was all he could manage.

"Zack?" CeeCee's voice came through, rich and sweet. "Are you ready for your treatment?"

"Uh-huh."

"Meet you at the whirlpool in ten minutes. Do you know where it is?"

Jack knew, but Zack shouldn't. "No."

"Through the courtyard to the left, past the laundry room, behind the gym."

"See you there."

Pulse bumping with anticipation, he raced to the bedroom, jammed himself into his new Speedo for his new persona, and mentally reminded himself of his goal. *Win her over. But slowly. In fact, make her work for it.*

7

The minute Zack sauntered into the steamy, fern-filled whirlpool pergola favoring his left knee, CeeCee's jaw hit the floor and her eyes rounded wide.

Most men would look ridiculous in a leopard-print Speedo. Jack wouldn't be caught dead in such swim trunks. But on Zack the tiny strip of material fit.

Perfectly.

He looked wild and masculine. With his washboard abs, and well-developed biceps, he flat put Alexander Skarsgard in *Tarzan* to shame.

From the time she was a small girl, she'd had a secret crush on Tarzan. A lingering jungle fantasy that included making love on a bed of banana tree leaves, but to heck with the King of the Apes. Zack Travis was the absolute sexiest thing she had ever clapped eyes on, and she was about to get into the whirlpool with him.

She wanted to ask him to pound his chest, throw back his head and do the Tarzan yell. Her toes curled at the notion. Last night had been no margarita-induced anomaly.

Bummeroo.

She'd hoped a good night's sleep and the stark light of day would help her see things clearly.

Apparently not. Inwardly, she groaned. It was official. Like it or not, she had the serious hots for Zack Travis.

Then again, what wasn't to like?

Great body, handsome face. Adventuresome, sexy, fun-loving, decidedly not marriage-minded, he was the perfect guy for her. They had a lot in common. Besides, what was so wrong with a red-hot fling?

It had been a long time since any man had moved her to this degree. The only one that even came close was the very one she refused to feel anything sexual toward.

His twin brother, Jack.

Zack closed the door behind him, then moved across the room to where she perched on the edge of the Jacuzzi, her feet dangling in the warm, bubbly water.

The closer he came, the harder it was to breathe. She peeked surreptitiously at him from lowered lashes. Despite his limp, he moved like a predatory cat on the hunt, nimble and smooth. He had a white towel, that contrasted sharply with his tanned skin, thrown over one shoulder.

She stared at the sinewy muscles bunched across his chest. Her pulse fluttered, as weightless and fast as hummingbird wings.

He stopped and peered down at her.

CeeCee felt his gaze igniting the top of her head, but she was too nervous to turn and meet his stare straight on.

The humidity in the room accentuated his scent. A fragrant masculine aroma, not cologne, she decided. Lighter, milder. Probably one of those zesty manly soaps.

His abdomen was chiseled; his belly button a provocative innie just begging to be tickled. His body hair swirled in a dark line that disappeared into the waist of the compact, low-slung swimsuit.

Her eyes grew even wider. The suit hid absolutely nothing.

Embarrassed, she spun her gaze across the room and focused on a Ficus plant in the corner.

She was so aware of him. His broad-shouldered presence encompassed the entire building. She wished that some other apartment dweller would pop inside to join them in the whirlpool and defuse the moment.

No such luck.

"How you doin'?" he drawled, his voice pushing through her like heated chocolate.

"Fine, fine."

"I had a great time last night."

"Me, too." She couldn't keep avoiding his eyes. Bravely, she raised her gaze, bracing herself for the head-on collision.

Whack!

Their eyes locked as they had the night before.

Steam rose around them in lazy, drifting curls. The water gurgled like smothered laughter. CeeCee felt flustered and girlish and completely out of her depth.

He was an unbelievably...virile male, no escaping it. Standing there in nothing but that skimpy spotted swimsuit, proud as the King of the Jungle, he was extravagant eye candy.

Thank heavens for that! Eye candy she could handle. No danger of her falling in love with eye candy. Because she certainly wasn't falling in love. No, siree. She might be riding the fast train to Lustland, but that was hunky-dory. Lust was fine.

Stop this, CeeCee. You're in charge here. You're the thera-pist. Take control.

She squared her shoulders. "Ease into the pool slowly," she commanded. "Hold on to the railing for support."

"*Oooh.* A forceful woman. I like that."

"We're here to heal your knee, Zack. Least you forget."

"Yes, ma'am," he said, not at all contritely, and settled himself beside her.

Their legs touched. Bare thigh against bare thigh. *Zip! Pop! Sizzle!*

The heat that swamped her body had nothing to do with the humidity in the closed confines and everything to do with her body's spontaneous reac-tion to Zack.

She wanted him, oh, yeah, but the intensity of her desire scared the stuffing out of her. She'd never expe-rienced anything like this raw, animal chemistry.

"What next?" he whispered.

"We get wet."

"Sounds good to me."

Good grief, the man could make the simplest statement sound like sexual innuendo.

CeeCee slid into the Jacuzzi and across to the other side, away from Zack. Her heart pounded and her face felt flushed. She tried desperately to convince herself it was due to the water temperature and nothing else. Heaven forbid she could keep her libido under wraps for a mere twenty-minute session in the whirlpool.

"We'll start by just sitting here a couple of minutes, letting our muscles relax."

"Whatever you say." He was looking at her lips now instead of trying to catch her eye.

"Why don't you tell me about winning the motocross championship," she suggested.

He shrugged. "Not much to tell."

CeeCee frowned. That didn't sound like most of the guys she knew. Ordinarily men loved bragging about sports and cars and things like that. Funny, Zack certainly didn't strike her as the modest type.

"Come on, don't be humble. Jack's told me you've won tons of contests. What kind of bike do you have?"

"Ducati."

Boy, getting him to talk about himself was like pulling teeth. Plus, he just kept staring at her. As if she were a succulent piece of fruit ripe for the picking. The more he studied her mouth, the more disconcerted she became, flicking out the tip of her tongue to moisten her lips.

She ducked her head, wanting to hide from him.

"Feels like a tropical island in here," he said.

"Uh-huh."

Stop looking at me!

"Reminds me of Hawaii."

"You've been to Hawaii?" Her head came up at that, and she managed to focus on his bearded chin which lent such a lawless quality to his appearance. "Which island?"

"Maui, Oahu, and Kauai. Never got around to the big island."

"You lucky dog," she breathed. "What was it? A motocross race?"

"Family vacation when Jack and I were kids."

"I've always wanted to go to Hawaii. It's a childhood dream of mine. In fact, both Jack and I separately entered a radio call-in contest to win a chance to visit Maui. K102 Houston is having a drawing to give away a free trip to Hawaii on the twenty-first."

"I'll keep my fingers crossed for you." He raised his crossed fingers.

"Thanks." She grinned. "I get goose bumps just thinking about going there."

"I'd love to be the one to take you for the first time." The longing in his voice startled her. Was the longing for Hawaii or her or both? The thought of lying on the beach with Zack in Hawaii stacked goose bumps on top of goose bumps until she felt like a goose bump sandwich.

"What's *your* secret dream?" She changed the subject as she struggled to regain her equilibrium.

"I've always wanted to skydive, but I've never gotten around to it."

"Me, too!"

"No? Really? Imagine that."

"Maybe we could go together sometime."

"Uh, maybe," he replied. "But not until my knee heals of course."

Was it her imagination or did he pale visibly beneath his beard? As if he were scared of skydiving. Nah. Couldn't be. This guy wasn't afraid of anything.

"Time for a few gentle stretches," she said, buffeted on all sides by unexpected feelings.

She wanted him and yet the power of her desire unnerved her. It was only sexual chemistry. She knew that, but it had been a very long time—if ever—since she'd felt anything quite like this.

She was forced to move closer. Her hands encircled his ankle and she carefully flexed then extended his leg.

"How does that feel?"

"Fine," he murmured.

"You have great musculature." She ran a hand up the back of his calf and her fingers caught fire.

"Why, thank you. I work out often."

"I think it has more to do with genetics. Jack's got the same calf muscles."

"Oh really? You've noticed?"

"Only in passing." She shrugged.

Ticktock.

Silence filled the room for a long moment, then Zack murmured, "You wouldn't have a secret thing for my brother, would you?"

"Gosh, no." She wasn't fibbing. Not really. She could have a thing for Jack if she let herself, but where a forever kind of guy was concerned, she kept her heart locked down tight.

"Are you sure? Are we in competition for your affections, CeeCee?"

She shook her head. "No. Jack understands that we can never be more than good friends."

"Does he?" Zack gave her an enigmatic stare. "Really?"

"Of course. He tells me everything about his life, and I tell him everything about mine."

"Everything? Do you give him a play-by-play of your dates like you would with a girlfriend?"

"Well, yeah. That's the beauty of our relationship."

"I think it stinks," he said bluntly.

"Excuse me?"

"My brother listens while you chatter away about

your encounters with other men?" Zack wagged an index finger. "You're a cruel one, CeeCee Adams. Teasing Jack with tales of your sexual antics. Whether you know it or not, you're driving him bonkers."

Was she?

Startled, she reflected on Zack's statement. Had she been tormenting Jack? When she needed a shoulder to cry on, Jack was always there for her. She'd never given his availability much thought beyond friendship.

Zack was correct. She had not only been unintentionally cruel, but selfish and blind to her faults as well. The realization stunned her.

Poor Jack. No wonder he'd snapped and issued her an ultimatum.

"And," Zack continued, "he's too much of a schmuck to do anything about it."

"Hey! Don't talk about Jack like that." Indignation replaced her shame.

"Don't get me wrong. I meant it in the nicest possible way. He's my brother and I love him, but he's a schmuck. He's got a fabulous babe like you living next door and he's never made a move?"

"Unlike you," she replied tartly, glaring at Zack. "Your brother is a perfect gentleman."

"In other words, he's *bor-ing*."

"No, he's not." Her emotions toggled from anger to regret to guilt and back again. "Jack is steady and dependable, tender and funny. He's a wonderful man."

"But you're the kind of woman who likes flashy cars, fancy parties, and naughty men."

Yes. No. Not exactly.

"What you'd really like," he continued huskily, "what you're secretly longing for, is a man to take charge. A man who'll let you know exactly what he wants from you. No ifs, ands, or buts about it."

"You don't know me well enough to say what I like."

"That's true." He narrowed his eyes, peering at her through half-lowered lids. "But I'd like to get to know you better. For instance, if I were to kiss you on the back of your neck, would you wriggle?"

"That's inappropriate," she said, but inside she thought, *oh yeah.*

JACK WAS CLAY IN HER HANDS. HER FINGERS kneaded his knee, massaging away the stiffness while at the same time sending tingles of awareness barreling straight up his leg and bursting into his groin.

Kiss her, man, Zack's voice urged inside his head,

but then Jack had a clearer, more rational thought. *Wait. Take your time. Let the tension escalate.*

CeeCee raised her head. Her eyes shone brightly. Tendrils of hair cleaved like a vine to her forehead, her cheek. She looked moist and dewy and ready for anything.

He clenched his jaw to stop a groan and knotted his hands into fists to keep from touching her. His gaze traced down her long neck to her slender collarbone and beyond. Her peach-size breasts swelled against the practical one-piece navy-blue swimsuit. This sensible suit was in sharp contrast to the teeny-weeny string bikini she'd had on last night, but it made no difference. The garment couldn't blot out her attributes.

Breasts of a goddess. Not too large, not too small. Just right. High and firm and round.

How he wanted her!

A shimmering furnace of heat blasted up his nerve endings. His nostrils flared as he inhaled deeply of her sweet, sexy scent mingling so intriguingly with the smell of chlorine.

With a blink of the eye he could picture her naked and in picturing her completely bare, tortured himself beyond endurance. His groin tightened, turned thick and heavy.

What was happening to him?

Normally he had excellent control over his more...er...baser instincts. If that wasn't the case, could he and CeeCee have remained just friends for so long? But playing the role of his twin brother was changing him in unexpected ways. He was becoming hungrier, less cautious, more willing to take a gamble to get what he wanted.

"Have you ever made love in a whirlpool?" She asked. She had stopped massaging him, although her hand was still at his knee.

Surprised, he gaped at her. Of course he'd never made love in a whirlpool. What was she suggesting? That they make love right here? Right now?

His pulse revved.

"I ask because Jack told me you've made love in exotic places all over the world."

Casually he shrugged, belying the pounding in his heart. "I don't like to brag about my romantic conquests. I'm not the type to kiss and tell."

Ha! That was a good one. Zack not bragging about his sexploits? That would be the day the earth stopped spinning. But the gentleman in Jack wouldn't allow him to emulate Zack in the bedroom. To Jack's way of thinking blabbing about his romantic encounters was not only crude but disrespectful to the lady in question.

"But have you made love in a hot tub?" CeeCee

repeated. Obviously, the subject intrigued her. "No need to name names."

"Sure. Hasn't everyone?"

"Not me," she whispered.

"Is this an invitation?" he asked huskily, reaching out to brush a curl from the side of her face.

"No." She shivered lightly.

A sharp sense of power surged through him knowing he had caused that response in her.

"At least not yet," she added.

"Not yet?" For one second, his heart stopped.

"I may not be interested in a relationship, but believe it or not, I don't hop into bed with just anyone who turns me on."

"And you think I do?" He placed a palm to his chest.

"Don't you?"

"No." He snorted.

"But Jack told me that you've had dozens and dozens of girlfriends."

"And he told me that you've had dozens and dozens of boyfriends."

"Touché."

"Hey, lady, just because I like to have fun and go out on lots of dates doesn't mean I'm easy." He tossed her a teasingly offended expression.

"I know! Everyone thinks the same thing about me." CeeCee laughed.

It was a rich, hearty sound that warmed him straight through his bones. "You'd think people could see beyond stereotypes, myself included."

"Exactly. Same here. Guilty as charged."

They laughed together, and it was a wonderful moment. The tension had dissipated. They enjoyed an easy camaraderie. The water was warm, the company fantastic. His knee didn't even hurt all that much. In that instant, Jack had an irresistible urge to come clean and tell her the truth.

But before he could weigh the wisdom of such a move, CeeCee flashed him a toothy grin, flicked out her tongue and ran it over her bottom lip. She was tormenting him, and she knew it.

The little minx.

Overcome, he realized he was going to have to kiss her. Angling his head, he leaned in so close their mouths were almost touching.

"Ahem." The clearing of a voice pulled them apart and drew their attention to the doorway.

"Excuse me, am I interrupting something?" Miss Abercrombie wore a high-cut gold lame French swimsuit even though she no longer had the figure to quite pull it off. Her hair was piled up on her head, held in place by a myriad of colorful bows. Muffin, as always, was clutched in her arms.

"No, not at all." CeeCee sprang from the water.

Before Jack could move, she'd already grabbed her robe and stuffed her feet into flip-flops.

Muffin barked.

"Shh," Miss Abercrombie hushed her dog and squinted at them. "Is that you, CeeCee dear? I'm not wearing my glasses."

"Yes, ma'am."

Muffin barked again her eyes trained on Jack and struggled to break free from Miss Abercrombie, her yelps growing louder.

"Is that Jack with you?" The elderly woman came closer. "Home from Mexico already, young man?"

"No." CeeCee pushed back her hair from her forehead with one hand in that carefree manner of hers that plucked at Jack's heartstrings. "This is Jack's identical twin brother, Zack. He's visiting for a few weeks while Jack is in Mexico. He...er, um, hurt his leg, and I was giving him physical therapy."

Miss Abercrombie grinned. "Oh, is that what you call it nowadays? In my time we used different terminology."

CeeCee's face flushed redder than her hair. Jack wanted to get out of the whirlpool, but he didn't want Miss Abercrombie to see him in the Speedo.

Muffin whined and pawed at Miss Abercrombie's arm.

"What's the matter with you, Muffin? That's not Jack," Miss Abercrombie scolded, then raised her head to address him.

"Do you mind if she has a little sniff of you? Just to let her know you're not your twin brother."

He was trapped! One sniff from meddlesome Muffin and his cover was blown.

The poodle leaped to the ground, trotted over to the hot tub, and hopped up on the edge beside Jack. Her little body trembled with excitement. She joyously licked his face.

"Will you look at that," he said, determined to plow his way through this. "She must think I'm Jack."

Miss Abercrombie came closer still and peered hard at him over the top of her glasses. "Muffin hates all men *except* Jack. Are you sure you're not Jack?"

He gulped and met the elderly lady's knowing stare. Laughing nervously, he cast a glance at CeeCee who was watching the whole episode with her hands cocked on her hips. Meanwhile, Muffin kept licking his earlobe like it was an ice cream cone.

"Of course I'm not Jack, although people have mixed us up a time or two. I'm a good five pounds thinner than my brother and I tan more easily than he does. And hey, look, I wear a beard and have longer hair."

Even he had to give a mental eye roll at that last comment, but he was desperate, grasping at straws. He couldn't have CeeCee finding out the truth this way. He wasn't going to be bested by Detective Muffin.

"You two look exactly alike," Miss Abercrombie mused.

He had the strangest feeling she was about to pry open his mouth and examine his teeth in her search for the truth. "We *are* identical twins."

"Well," CeeCee said, "I'll leave you two to discuss the miracle of Muffin liking two men. I've got things to do."

"Hey, wait!" Jack said, rising to get out of the hot tub.

But CeeCee just waved at him and headed for the door. "Meet you here tomorrow at six after I get off work. Is that okay?"

"Great," he muttered. This had not turned out the way he had planned.

The minute CeeCee left, he found Miss Abercrombie studying his Tarzan getup with a suspicious eye.

"Uh, hi." He lifted a hand.

"Don't you hi me, Jack Travis. I want to know why

you've got CeeCee convinced that you're your own twin brother and I want to know now."

There was no fooling Muffin or Miss Abercrombie. He might as well come clean. In fact, Jack realized, it might do him a world of good to share his secret. It never hurt to have an ally.

He cast a glance to the door, making sure CeeCee was gone, then lowered his voice. "Promise me you won't tell CeeCee."

Miss Abercrombie looked skeptical. "I can't promise that. Why are you trifling with the woman's affections? That's not like you, Jack."

"Miss Abercrombie, this is very important. I promise you the last thing I want to do is hurt her. In fact, I'm in love with her."

"Well, why didn't you say so?" Miss Abercrombie smiled gleefully. "I'll even help play matchmaker. I always thought you two would be perfect together."

8

For the next three weeks he and CeeCee bonded like hydrogen and oxygen. Coming together for those short, sweet twenty-minute intervals every evening where they teased and coaxed, massaged and stroked.

Moving ever closer to a deeper intimacy.

But at times it was tough keeping up his ruse. On many occasions, Jack had to push through his natural reticence and tap into his own wild side. He flirted outrageously with CeeCee and he touched her often. Before she went to bed every night, he called her on the phone and said uninhibited things that were just this side of phone sex.

With each passing day, the tension mounted.

He was wound tighter than a roll of surgical tape. Taut with anticipation. Hungry to make love to her.

Because whether CeeCee would admit it to herself or not, she was falling for him. He could tell by the way her eyes lit up when she saw him. She looked the way he felt inside. Like Christmas had come early every time she walked into a room.

His fantasies kept him awake at night, tossing and turning with sweat. Fantasies that made his heart swell with yearning. The only thing he'd ever wanted as much as he wanted CeeCee was to become a doctor.

Well, he was a doctor now.

But he'd yet to become CeeCee's lover.

He only had one more week to wrangle her into his bed. One more week to convince her that she could fall in love and stay in love for a lifetime. One more week to prove her ridiculous family curse was nothing but a self-fulfilling prophecy.

The clock was ticking. Time for phase two of his "debunk the family whammy" plan. Time to accelerate this slow seduction. Time to consummate this simmering tension before they both went off the deep end.

She'd called him last night and told him she would stop by after work to shore up last-minute instructions for the bachelor charity auction the following afternoon. He'd almost forgotten about the darned thing until she brought it up.

Meaning his Friday night and Saturday afternoon would be taken up by some socialite rich enough to outbid the others for the privilege of hanging out with Motocross Champion Zack "Wild Man" Travis on Galveston Island.

He called his twin again but got no answer and left a voice mailing telling him there was no reason for him to show up. The bachelor auction was taken care of. Still he worried. What if his brother didn't the get the message and he came straight to Houston?

You're obsessing, he assured himself. Zack would get the message.

At that moment he heard the distinctive noise of CeeCee's car engine pulling into the parking lot. Jerking open his front door, he hurried out to greet her.

"Hey, beautiful," he called.

"Hi, handsome." She breezed over, carrying a garment bag. How he wished he could bottle that smile to carry in his pocket whenever he was away from her!

She looked so gorgeous he couldn't speak for a full sixty seconds. She gazed at him. The wind tossed her curls against the smooth curve of her cheek. Her green eyes held a hint of mischief.

"Here's your tuxedo for the bachelor auction tomorrow."

He just stared, taking her in and thinking, *I'm going to give you all the love I have to give. I'm going to convince you that your life is charmed, not cursed. I'm going to help you see that you can have your heart's desire.*

"Zack?" She dangled the tux from its wooden hanger.

"Huh, oh, yeah." He took the garment bag from her. "Are you coming over to fill me in on the details of the auction?"

"Sure. Just let me go change first."

He jerked a thumb at his apartment. "You know I was about to throw a steak on the grill. Would you like to join me?"

Man, he was getting good at telling these white lies. He'd been marinating the steak, tossing a salad and baking potatoes for the last hour, waiting for her to show up.

"Sounds great. I'm starved."

"You like your steak rare, right?"

"How did you know?"

He went silent a moment, realizing he'd slipped. Zack had no idea how CeeCee liked her steaks cooked. "Um, you just seem like a rare woman."

"You're pretty glib." She laughed.

"A special talent of mine." He gave her a little salute, one of Zack's trademarks gestures.

"See you in a few," she said and went to her apartment.

Lord, the woman had the most perfect tush in the entire universe, bar none. Tonight, he was going to kiss her again. Although there'd been a lot of caressing and deep eye gazing these past three weeks, he hadn't kissed her since the night he'd come back from Mexico.

He had wanted to wait, but he'd reached the end of his rope. He couldn't wait any longer. Tonight, he was going to kiss her silly and let nature take its course.

Slipping back into his apartment, he hung up the tux, and then hurried to the kitchen to grab the steaks from the fridge. He stepped out onto the thumbnail-size patio and slapped the tenderloins on the grill.

He felt keyed-up, twisted in knots. Perspiration beaded his brow; he swiped it away with a forearm. Closing his eyes, he took a deep breath.

Stop freaking out.

But his insides were syrup as he thought about kissing CeeCee again and what might come after the kissing. His gut tightened. Would tonight be the night they made love?

"Need any help?"

At the sound of CeeCee's sexy voice, he jumped a foot and his eyes flew open. She lounged in the doorway between the kitchen and the patio, a vision of loveliness. Her hair, freshly brushed, cascaded over her shoulders like a red-hot lava flow. She wore a pair of well-worn, denim shorts, thin white sandals, and a blue cotton sleeveless blouse.

She sauntered out onto the patio smelling of the tropics—all pineapple and banana and coconut. She perched on the edge of the hip-high rock wall separating his pathetic patio from the apartment next door and gently swung her so-fabulous legs.

Jack strategically held the empty steak platter in front of his lower anatomy, desperately trying to camouflage his reaction.

Come on. Say something Zackish. Be bold. Take charge. Act!

But he could only stare, dumbstruck by her beauty. Before he could think of anything remotely interesting to say, his phone rang.

"Could you hand me my cell?" he asked from where he manned the grill, happy to have a distraction. His phone was on the small wrought iron bistro table situated between them.

"Sure." CeeCee hopped off the half-wall and sauntered to the table as if she were wading through melted butter.

The charm bracelet at her wrist jangled as she picked up his phone on the second ring. She glanced down. "It's from K102 radio."

"Gimme." With the tongs in one hand, he reached for his phone with the other.

She passed it over.

He pressed "accept" on the third ring and put it on speaker. "Hello?"

"Hello! Hello! Hello!" replied a rapid-fire, enthusiastic voice. "This is Ron Tipman from K102."

"You won! You won!" CeeCee squealed and bounced around the patio like a pogo stick. "Oh my gosh, they called!"

Jack grinned. He'd entered the contest to win a trip to Hawaii for CeeCee. Her delight sent him straight over the moon. He couldn't wait to see her face when they stepped off the plane in Maui. Volcanoes in the background, palm trees swaying in the foreground.

"If you can just tell me that your name is indeed Jack Travis of 198 River Run, you will have won an all-expense paid trip for two to Maui, Hawaii!"

"What?" His gut clenched.

"Sir," the disc jockey said, "are you Jack Travis?"

"Uh, well..."

Was he Jack Travis? He looked from CeeCee to the phone and back again.

"Remember, sir," the disc jockey prompted, "you must show valid identification to claim the prize. So if you lie, it's going to work."

CeeCee's face fell like a fractured plate.

He *could* prove he was Jack Travis, but not now, not today. Oh hell, why had the radio station called when CeeCee just happened to be here with him stuck on speakerphone?

If he told a lie, he'd lose the trip.

If he told the truth, at least at this point, he would lose CeeCee.

And he couldn't let that happen. Not when he was so close to winning her heart.

"Sir?"

"No," Jack croaked at last; he could feel the heat of CeeCee's gaze on his face. "I'm not Jack Travis."

"That's too bad, sir. I'm sorry."

"But Jack's my twin brother. I could contact him, have him call you."

"I'm afraid not. The rules state he had to be home to get the qualifying call. But keep listening to K102," the disc jockey said, then hung up.

"Rats!" CeeCee exclaimed. "Jack will be so disappointed he missed the call."

He's only disappointed because he couldn't win the trip

for you, CeeCee, don't you realize that? Now he was thinking about himself in third person. Messed up.

"Sorry, I couldn't fake it."

"It wasn't your fault."

"You deserve to go first class to Hawaii."

"Oh, Zack, that's so nice of you, but deserve it too."

"I'm not being nice," he growled. "I'm thinking of you wearing a grass skirt and coconut shells for a bra and swinging those hips of yours in time to 'Tiny Bubbles.'"

She boldly met his gaze. "Only if you wear those Tarzan swim trunks and swing from a Banyan tree."

"You've got yourself a deal, Lucille."

"Check the steaks." She laughed, not taking him the least bit seriously. "They look done."

His frustration over not winning the trip passed, but Jack still couldn't shake his nagging conscience. He'd seriously begun questioning the wisdom of the masquerade, even though Zack's Crock-Pot slow seduction had been progressing nicely with CeeCee. He felt pulled in two directions, and neither course was safe.

"The steaks were great," CeeCee enthused as they sat at the patio table, surrounded by empty plates. "But you're not fooling me. You didn't just happen to have an extra filet mignon and baked potato lying around."

"You got me," he confessed. "I'd been wanting to do something nice for you, to say thanks for the physical therapy but I was afraid to ask you out on a date. I didn't want to be too pushy."

"I appreciate that." She grinned. "But if you'd have asked, I wouldn't have turned you down."

"Oh really? Then how about tomorrow night? We could grab a bite to eat, head out to the speedboat races."

"You can't."

"What?"

"Have you forgotten already? You'll be in Galveston with your charity auction date."

"Why don't you bid on me?" He leaned closer and gave her Zack's best grin.

"Well, first of all it's against the rules for the coordinator to bid in the auction, but mostly you're out of my price range."

"What are you talking about?"

"Wait and see." She winked in a way that sent a fissure of pure heaven sparking through him. "You're a top draw. Advance ticket sales have skyrocketed since it was announced you were going on the auction block."

"No kidding?"

"Face it. You're hot stuff, Zack Travis." She swung her leg back and forth under the table. She'd kicked off her sandals earlier and her foot grazed his shin. Her pupils widened at the contact.

Although he thought her touch had been accidental at first, it was no accident when she took those toes and ran them from his knee to his ankle.

"CeeCee." He leaned in close and whispered softly into her ear. "What are you doing?"

"Who me?" She feigned an innocent expression.

"You're fooling with fire, lady."

"Am I?"

"You don't want to get me started."

"Why not?"

"I might have a hard time stopping."

"Oh, yeah?" Her jaunty eyes glistened.

"Yeah."

He tugged her from her chair and pulled her into his lap.

"Oh." CeeCee inhaled deeply and stared into his face.

Her heart revved. She'd decided that three weeks was long enough. She was about to explode from the sexual chemistry seething between them. She'd come over here tonight hoping they would finally end up in bed together. Her choice of short shorts had been no accident. Nor had her cologne—*Forbidden Sin*— been a careless afterthought.

"You're so bad," she murmured.

She was ready for anything he could dish out. She'd gotten to know him well enough to realize they could indeed have a terrific time without either of them getting hurt.

He pressed his heated mouth to hers. His tongue —oh heavenly days—better than ambrosia and champagne and chocolate all rolled into one. He licked her lips with quick flicks of that incredible tongue, then traced the outline of her teeth. He drew her bottom lip between his teeth and sucked gently.

Greedily she kissed him back with an overwhelming, ravenous desire. The strength of her passion almost bowling her over so unbelievable was the aching need growing inside her.

She leaned into him and cocked her head slightly to grant him easier access to her mouth. She splayed her hands across his chest, thirstily drinking from his lips.

The tingling started in her breasts, but it swiftly

spread, heating her skin, skipping along synapses, ending up a tight ball of electrical impulses many inches below her waist.

He pulled away a moment, her lips bereft at his parting. He looked deeply into her eyes and threaded his fingers through the loose tendrils of hair trailing along her shoulder.

She reached out to stroke the silk of his beard. Their gazes stayed locked. She heard her pulse beating in her ears.

There was no mistaking the degree of his desire for her. His hardness was both flattering and exciting. He spanned her waist with his hands, then kissed her again.

His muscled chest crushed her breasts, but it wasn't unpleasant. Her nipples ached sweetly, rising up to press against him. When he shifted, his movements abraded her nipples through the thin material of her blouse, causing her to gasp out loud.

She inhaled him like oxygen. His tongue delved deeper. She moaned into his mouth, riding the crest of intoxicating sensation until CeeCee didn't think she could stand one minute more not being merged with him.

His mouth was on her throat now, his tongue licking little swirls of heat that only served to send her over the edge, deeper and deeper into impending oblivion.

"Oh, Jack," she moaned.

And everything stopped.

Zack stopped moving, stopped kissing her, stopped stroking her skin with his fingers. She could have bitten off her tongue when she realized she'd called him by his twin brother's name.

"W-what?" he whispered. "What did you call me?"

CeeCee pulled back, expecting to see disappointment etched on his face, but oddly enough another emotion flickered in the depths of his chocolate-brown eyes.

Was that happy surprise?

She must be mistaken. Besides, the look was gone.

Gently he settled her back into her own chair, their sudden passion dissipating like a spent balloon.

"I'm sorry, Zack, so sorry. It was a simple slip of the tongue. I'm just so used to Jack being around that I accidentally called his name."

"While you're kissing me? Sure it wasn't a Freudian slip?" Jack held his breath as he waited for her answer. "Would you rather be with my brother?"

"'Course not." Her voice rose slightly on the denial.

"You've got sexual feelings for Jack?" He finally dared to speak the words.

"No." She shook her head as if trying to convince herself as well as him.

"You're certain?"

"Don't worry, Zack." She knotted a fist over his chest and sent rivers of heat shaking through him. "You're the one I'm attracted to. Not your brother."

Jack's hopes dropped.

Kersplat!

That's what he got for perpetuating this dangerous charade. This dungeon of his own construction. He was hearing the truth whether he liked it or not. But he and Zack were one and the same. If she loved one dimension of himself, she had to love the other.

Right?

"Zack...I really am sorry."

"There's nothing to apologize for." He forced cheerfulness into his voice and shrugged. "I've called out the wrong name at the wrong moment myself."

"It would probably be better if I went home." She started to rise to her feet.

"Wait." He reached out and wrapped his hand around her slender wrist and came into contact with her charm bracelet.

The damn bracelet that reminded her why she

would always have to pick guys like Zack over guys like him.

"Yes?"

Their eyes met again. He wanted him. No mistaking that sultry look.

"Take this with you," he said, then kissed her within an inch of her life.

❧ 9 ❧

CeeCee tried not to stare but it was downright impossible what with Zack decked out in that black tuxedo, red tie, and matching cummerbund. Not to mention the blood-red rosebud tucked into his lapel.

He looked like someone straight off the set of *The Bachelor*.

They were standing in the hospital corridor that led to the auditorium where the bachelor auction was due to start in fifteen minutes. Zack looked completely different than he had for the past three weeks. Plus, his limp had almost vanished.

In this moment, except for that neatly trimmed beard, he looked exactly like Jack.

Her heart gave a strange hop. She asked herself,

not for the first time, who she was really attracted to. Her wild fling-waiting-to-happen or his steady twin.

CeeCee forced her gaze off Zack and onto the clipboard in her hand. She stifled a yawn. She had slept poorly, thanks to what had *not* happened in Jack's apartment the night before.

Each time she had dozed off she would jerk awake a few minutes later, soaked in perspiration and tingling all over from the vestiges of a steamy dream where Zack was the starring attraction.

At dawn, she'd given up trying to sleep and had instead proceeded to worry herself sick about the auction. It was her first time hosting such an event, and she was desperate for things to go smoothly.

Of course with Zack as the headliner, what could possibly go wrong?

Women fainting in a fervor over him?

Men getting jealous and busting his chops?

Kids chasing after him for an autograph?

Okay, tons of things could go wrong.

"Um, you've got something poking out of your dress," he said.

"What?" Distracted, she reached around to feel a price tag sticking up from her zipper.

"Hold on, sweetheart. I'll deal with that pesky tag."

And then his fingers were on her skin, burning a searing path straight to her groin.

Oh gosh, they were going to have to do something about this sexual tension. Before her panties spontaneously burst into flames. Before she melted into a puddle and evaporated. Before...

Never mind that, Adams. Head in the game.

The sooner they got their affair rolling, the sooner the sparks would sizzle then fizzle, and the sooner things could get back to normal. But she couldn't have Zack until Sunday. He would belong to the lucky lady who outbid all the others for a date in Galveston with him.

In the meantime, she would have to put all sexy thoughts on hold.

"Got it." Zack tucked the errant tag into his pocket, his grin so endearing, she almost absconded with him back to her apartment.

What the heck was the matter with her? Yesterday, when she could have made love to him, she had chickened out and run away.

Why?

And why did the thought of those man-starved single society women bidding on him at the charity auction make her blood run cold?

Sheesh, she was losing it.

She didn't want him to strut his stuff before other women. She didn't want to hear them ooh and aah over him. She didn't want him to go off with anyone else.

But she couldn't bid on him, and she couldn't spirit him away from the event. The auction normally raised thousands of dollars in funds for health care programs to benefit inner-city kids. She couldn't put her own desires above children.

She'd have to tough it out and pray Zack didn't start a fling with the lady who paid big bucks for a date with him.

The bad thing was, tomorrow was her twenty-eighth birthday and she'd be spending it alone without either Jack or Zack.

"Here," she said, tucking her clipboard under her arm and giving Zack a last-minute once-over. "Your tie is a little crooked." She reached out to adjust it.

He grinned down at her.

"Oh, my *gawd*!" a female voice shrieked. "That's Zack Travis! Isn't he just the bomb?"

Another girl squealed in response. The next thing CeeCee knew they were knee-deep in teenage girls giggling and blushing and asking Zack to sign their T-shirts.

Tsk, tsk, what a spectacle.

I won't get jealous. I won't! It's just showbiz and the attention is good for the auction.

Besides, she had no call for jealousy. She had no claim on Zack, nor he on her. And that's exactly the way she wanted it.

Wasn't it?

"Sorry, ladies," she said, firmly taking Zack by the arm and detaching him from one leggy blonde with a skirt so small she could have used it as an eye patch. "I've got to get him backstage."

He shrugged helplessly at the teenagers, and one even had the audacity to hiss at CeeCee.

Brat!

She hustled him through the back door to the auditorium. "I've got a few things to take care of. You be good while I'm gone."

"Sweetheart," he murmured, leaning in close.

So close the hairs on the back of her neck stood on end.

"I'm always good. Just you wait and see."

"You're impossible," she said, torn between being irritated with him and being very turned on by his hand lingering at her waist.

"Oh, no. That's where you're wrong. I'm very, very possible. Especially when it comes to you, my flame-haired vamp."

"Quit it!" She moved away, unable to stop a warm flush from spreading up her neck. "I'll be back in a few to check on you."

"Bye." He gave her a goofy grin and wriggled both his fingers and his eyebrows.

Why did she have the feeling she was going to come back to find half a dozen women feeding him grapes and fanning him with tree fronds?

Because that's the kind of guy he is, CeeCee. Face facts. Mr. Footloose and Fancy-Free may not come with strings attached, but for that very reason you can't expect him to have eyes for only you.

But dammit, that's exactly what she did expect!

She was confused about her feelings for Zack. Very confused.

Could things possibly get any more snarled between him and CeeCee?

Jack leaned against the wall considering that question. While his plan to impersonate his brother might have looked good at the onset, the deeper he slipped into the deception, the harder he found it to look himself in the mirror.

Hang on. Not much longer. You're almost there.

"Mr. Travis?"

A soft, feminine voice brought his head up. Three young women sidled up to him, each clutching glossy eight-by-ten photographs of Zack.

"May we have your autograph?" The boldest one tentatively extended a picture and pen toward him.

All three looked so excited with awestruck gazes on their faces, and he didn't have the heart to send them away.

"Sure, sure." He smiled. "What's your name?"

"Suzie."

He scribbled, "To Suzie of the amazing blue eyes" across the bottom of the photo, then added Zack's signature.

"Thank you so much," she breathed, blushed prettily, and stepped back to let her friends come forward.

The next thing he knew, he was surrounded by women—tall ones, short ones, old ones, young ones. Blondes and brunettes and redheads. All of them seeking to talk to him, touch him, flirt with him. They batted their eyes and asked him about himself. They offered to cook him dinner or take him for a ride in their cars. They oohed and aahed, cooed and simpered.

Jack had never received this kind of female adoration, and it disconcerted him. He felt claustrophobic and ached to bolt from the room. But how could he? These women would be bidding on him, supporting the auction. If he were rude, it would take money from CeeCee's worthy charity.

He forced himself to smile and joke, to say something nice to every one of them, but it wasn't easy. He drew on everything he knew about his charming brother and used it to maximum effect—the endearing grin, the lazy drawl, the flirtatious wink.

Zack might enjoy being the center of women's attention, but Jack found out rather quickly that he did not. There was only one woman he wanted fawning after him, only one woman he wanted to kiss for the rest of his natural days. Only one woman who made his heart beat faster and his breathing quicken.

The woman standing in the doorway, arms crossed over her chest, looking mad enough to chew nails.

"What's going on in here?" CeeCee snapped, drilling Jack with a bone-chilling glare. "No one's allowed backstage except employees and the bachelors. Shoo, ladies. Go on. You can bid on Mr. Travis to your heart's content when the auction begins."

Jack watched the disappointed women file out the door, but then he turned his smile on CeeCee. No point wasting the charm he'd gone to so much trouble milking up.

"Hey, babe." He winked.

"I thought I told you to be good," she chided.

"All I did was sign a few autographs. No harm done."

"Women follow you like a trail of ants to cookie crumbs." CeeCee shook her head, but she was smiling. He took that as a positive sign.

"I didn't invite them back here," he said. "They just sniffed me out."

"Must be your cologne. What is it? Eau d' Harem?"

"Nah, Scent of a Rebel."

"Gets 'em every time."

"You know that's right."

"Zack," she said at the very moment he said, "CeeCee."

They both chuckled.

"You go first," he said.

"No, you."

"I don't want you to think it means anything when I flirt with other women," he said. "Because it doesn't."

She shrugged. "Makes no never mind to me."

"You're not the least bit jealous?"

"Not a bit."

"Not even a teeny-weeny little bit?" He marked off an inch with his thumb and index finger."

"Not even a speck."

She laughed again and shook her head. He couldn't help tracing his gaze along her body. She looked fabulous in that sparkly blue dress with the cinched waist. Her three-inch heels made her almost as tall as he.

Dammit, he wanted her to be jealous. He wanted her to fight for him. Then before he realized what he was doing, Jack kissed her.

His arm snaked around that gorgeous twenty-four-inch waist.

Deny this!

He hauled her flush against his chest and caught her wrists with one hand. His mouth captured those red-hot lips.

Just try and pretend you don't want more, princess!

Jack kissed her hard and deep, with an urgency that vibrated up from the core of him. Her body heat penetrated his psyche on a primitive level, excited him beyond belief.

She sagged into him.

Desire shot through his body like a heat-seeking missile. He reached up and traced a finger over her soft-as-silk cheek.

In just a few minutes a horde of hungry women would be bidding on him, vying for the honor of taking him to Galveston Island. But Jack didn't want any of them. He only wanted CeeCee.

He looked into her eyes, saw her staring up at him, alarm on her endearing features. Immediately she drew back.

"I got lipstick all over your face," she said huskily. "And here I am without a tissue."

From his pocket, he produced a handkerchief.

"You're just like Jack." She dabbed at his cheek, studiously avoiding his gaze. "Never without a clean hankie."

But I am Jack, he longed to tell her. I'm the one giving you toe-curling kisses, not Zack.

Go ahead, tell her.

He opened his mouth to speak the truth but at that moment five tuxedoed bachelors strolled through the door and the opportunity was lost.

NOW SHE KNEW WHY THEY CALLED HIM WILD Man. You could never tell what he might do.

CeeCee fingered her lips. Truthfully, her knees were still a little shaky as the aftermath of Zack's kiss lingered in her system, rending her almost useless.

The auditorium was packed, the attendees anxiously awaiting the bachelor auction. She should be battling stage-fright butterflies. Instead, all she could think about was kissing Zack. What was going on here? She had kissed dozens of handsome men. She'd even had a fling or two. Jack was her only regret, but ever since Zack had come along, she'd gone all gooey-headed over him.

Not a good sign.

Her pulse whirled like a helicopter blade whenever she chanced to look at him. In his form-fitting tux, he overshadowed every other bachelor behind the velvet curtain. But it wasn't the tuxedo that lent him his sexual attraction.

No, siree.

Even if he'd been in a pair of cutoff blue jeans and a ratty T-shirt, he would have outshone every other man there. She knew exactly what he looked like under those fancy duds. She had been giving him physical therapy in the whirlpool. Except for his brother, in CeeCee's eyes, there was none finer than Zack Travis.

And apparently more than a hundred women in the audience chanting, "Wild Man, Wild Man, Wild Man," shared her opinion.

The jealousy she'd earlier denied stormed into her throat, making it hard to breathe. She couldn't believe that he would be leaving with some other woman this afternoon.

An irritating tic jumped in her left eye. This was crazy. She had to snap out of envy mode. She had a benefit to host. CeeCee clasped and unclasped her hands. Then she threw back her shoulders, held her head high, and stalked onstage. She reached the podium, took the microphone in her hand, and then began to tell the crowd about the charity.

The audience settled down, but only slightly. CeeCee introduced the auctioneer, then moved back into the wings to watch the proceedings.

They had saved the best for the end. Zack was the last bachelor on the program. When he strolled onstage and the auctioneer called his name and began describing his attributes, she could practically see the wallets opening and money pouring out.

From across the platform, Zack's eyes searched and found hers. He gave her a wink. A wink that snagged her heart.

Oh! CeeCee thought. *I'm getting into something I can't handle.*

"Let's start the bidding at five hundred dollars," the auctioneer said. "After all, we are talkin' one mighty sexy motocross champ."

"Six hundred," a familiar voice rang out.

CeeCee shielded her eyes and peered into the crowd. Was that Janet's voice?

"Seven hundred!"

"Eight hundred."

"Nine hundred."

It *was* Janet! Her best girlfriend was bidding on the guy *she* wanted to have a fling with? CeeCee glowered. How could she do this to her? Janet knew how much she liked Zack. She gritted her teeth and slowly began to shred her copy of the program into tiny little pieces.

"One thousand dollars."

Shred.

Zack gave the audience a Cary Grant smile and tossed his head like a fashion model, working them up.

The rascal.

Shred. Shred.

"Eleven hundred." Janet again.

CeeCee could see her statuesque friend standing up in the front row waving her hand. The eye tic was back, jumping uncontrollably.

"Twelve hundred."

"Thirteen."

"Two thousand!" Janet shouted.

Shred. Shred. Shred. Too bad the paper wasn't Janet's throat.

"Twenty-one hundred."

The bids flew so fast the auctioneer could barely keep up. She had known Zack was popular, she just hadn't realized how many women would be willing to spend so much money simply to spend thirty-six hours with him at a cute bed-and-breakfast on Galveston Island.

The lucky dogs.

"Twenty-five hundred," Janet shouted.

Good grief! Did her friend have no shame? The highest any of the other bachelors had gone for was eighteen hundred dollars. What was the matter with Janet? Why did she want Zack so badly? Hurt feelings replaced her resentment. Yes, she'd known she what she was up against from other women when it came to Zack, she just hadn't expected to compete with her friend.

Zack seemed delighted by the whole thing. He kept strutting around the stage like a prize peacock, preening and striking macho poses that had the crowd in gales of laughter. CeeCee was ready to trot over and kick him in the behind. His ego desperately needed downsizing.

And she was just the woman to do it. Unfortunately, she'd have to wait until he returned from his date on Monday.

Argh!

Patience wasn't her strongest virtue.

Shred. Shred. Hey, she was out of paper.

CeeCee looked down at the snowstorm of paper

flecks surrounding her. Pathetic! It was the sexual tension making her so crazed. That was all. If she'd slept with him and gotten him out of her system, she wouldn't give two hoots in the wind who was bidding on him.

"Sold for three thousand dollars to the leggy brunette in the front row!" the auctioneer shouted.

Janet bounced with joy.

CeeCee's stomach plummeted to her feet. Janet had won Zack. Then to her horror, her eyes went misty.

What was the matter with her? She didn't get weepy over men. Not ever. Well, except the tears she'd shed over losing Jack's friendship. But she shouldn't care about a short-term romance that had never even progressed beyond kissing.

She wanted to flee, get away before she had to face either Zack or Janet. But her assistant, Deirdre, appeared at her elbow, an excited look on her face. "We've raised ten thousand dollars," she whispered.

Yes. Well, that was great. She had to go to the podium and announce the details to the audience. It was the last thing she wanted to do, the last place she wanted to be, but CeeCee sucked up her disappointment and strode out to deliver the closing speech. The bachelors and their dates were lined up across the stage, eagerly waiting her news.

LORI WILDE

By some miracle she managed to come off sounding polished and professional. Finally, she was able to escape, only to be stopped in the hall by Janet's voice.

"CeeCee! Wait."

She tried to hurry outside. Tried hard to pretend she hadn't heard. She picked up the pace and threw the heavy exit door open. She burst out into the bright sunlight. She stood there blinking, and then the damned door slammed on the tail of her dress.

Before she could jerk herself free, Janet tugged open the door and gaped at her. "Where are you rushing off to? Didn't you hear me calling you?"

"Uh, was that you?"

Great. Now Janet was going to rub her face in her victory. She turned to find Zack and Janet arm in arm and grinning like a pair of opossums.

"What is it?" CeeCee asked, feeling exceedingly tired.

They looked good together. Both tall and dark. If she were a bigger person, she'd give them her blessings. Instead, she wanted to wring both their necks.

"Happy birthday to you," Janet began to sing and thrust Zack forward.

"It's not my birthday." CeeCee felt quarrelsome.

"It is tomorrow," Zack said.

"Happy birthday to you," Janet kept singing.

Zack reached out and took CeeCee's hand. "Pack your bags, lady, we're off to Galveston."

"I don't get it."

"Your birthday present." Janet waved at Zack with a flourish of her hand. "*Ta-da.*"

CeeCee frowned. "Will you two please just tell me what's going on?"

"Since the foundation's rules prohibited the coordinator from bidding on the auction items, Janet and I cooked up this little scheme."

CeeCee stared at Zack. "You mean you rigged the auction?" She turned to Janet. "You weren't really bidding on him?"

"I was bidding on him for you, silly. Did you actually think I'd try to steal your guy?" Janet shook her head.

"Who's shelling out the three grand?" CeeCee asked.

"I am." Zack grinned. "It's for a good cause, and hey, I needed the tax deduction."

"You mean you paid three thousand for a date with me?" She placed a hand to her chest, flattered, but suddenly apprehensive.

"Yes," he admitted, a certain glimmer in his eyes that looked far too much like the way Jack had looked at her the day he had given her the ultimatum.

Oh my gosh, what did that mean?

If Zack was forking out three thousand dollars for her birthday present, he must be more serious about her than she thought and that scared CeeCee more than a million beautiful supermodels screaming, "Wild Man, Wild Man, Wild Man."

❧ 10 ❧

Jack and CeeCee strolled arm in arm down the Galveston seawall at sunset. He was dressed in black jeans and a print silk shirt. She wore a siren-red sheath dress that threatened to stop his pulse.

People passing by, most of them in swimsuits or shorts, gave them the once-over. Who could blame them for staring? She was with the most gorgeous creature on the face of the earth and he knew it.

Overhead, seagulls cawed and glided gently on the breeze. The air tasted salty and smelled of delicious aromas emanating from the restaurants lining the street. Couples and families pedaled surreys around them. The young and the young at heart whizzed by on in-line skates. Souvenir shops beckoned from the sidelines, offering seashells and brightly colored trinkets.

But Jack couldn't stop looking at CeeCee. She was chattering about anything and everything—the auction, the weather, how nice it had been of he and Janet to arrange this for her birthday.

He hung on her every word, but he was so dazzled by her beauty, he forgot what she had just said. Occasionally she would turn toward him, tilt her head in that endearing way of hers, and smile at him like he held the key to the universe.

It was a powerful feeling.

He couldn't believe he actually had her all to himself. No friends or co-workers around. No Muffin or Miss Abercrombie to interrupt.

For the next day and a half they would be alone together. They were staying at a turn-of-the-century Victorian style bed-and-breakfast on The Strand and even though they had separate rooms, there was an adjoining door.

Things were going so right he scarcely dared admit it. One false move could upset the delicate balance. He had to tread lightly while at the same time doing everything in his power to win her heart.

His hopes soared. He had the evening planned to the tiniest detail. An extravagant candlelight dinner at Guido's, a moonlight jaunt across the ferry, a horse-drawn carriage ride back to their bed-and-breakfast. He'd already arranged with the inn owner to have rose petals sprinkled across CeeCee's bed, a bottle of champagne on ice, and a tray of chocolate-covered strawberries. The whole thing had cost him a mint, but it didn't matter.

Nothing was too good for his CeeCee.

"Oh, look, Zack, a po'boy stand." She stopped beside a six-by-six-foot wooden hut, dispensing fried shrimp poor boy sandwiches and greasy curly fries. "I haven't had one of those since I was a kid and my third stepfather Ernie used to bring us here. Can we get one?"

"But what about dinner?"

She waved a hand. "Who wants to sit in some stuffy old restaurant when we can plunk down right here on the seawall and have a shrimp po'boy with lots of tartar sauce."

"We've got reservations." He glanced at his watch.

"Goodness," she said. "If you're that set on the restaurant then okay, but I gotta tell you, you're acting a whole lot like your brother and not a bit like the Wild Motorcycle Man."

"Am I?" he murmured.

"Oh, you know Jack. He plans everything to the

nth degree. Not that it's bad, mind you, but he's not very spontaneous." She lowered her voice as if revealing a secret. "Like he'd never blow off dinner reservations for a curbside po'boy."

"Shrimp po'boy it is," Jack said firmly, her comment stinging a little. Did she really consider him that dull? But when CeeCee leaned into him, her breasts crushed against his chest, he forgot about everything except pleasing her.

Remember, lunkhead, act like Zack.

He stepped up to the vendor and ordered two sandwiches to go.

"Get us some fries and a couple of root beers, too," CeeCee said. "No wait. Just get one big root beer with two straws. We can share."

After he'd paid for the order, CeeCee took the bag from him, pulled out a French fry, and nibbled on it gracefully.

"This way." She guided him to the edge of the seawall, kind of dancing as she went, and away from the bulk of foot traffic. She plunked down on the cement, kicked off her shoes, and let them tumble to the sand some three feet below.

He shook his head, bewildered and bemused by her ability to turn anything into a lark. Jack stood there a moment, not sure what to do next, but when she turned those inquiring green eyes on him, he followed suit. He planted himself firmly beside her, then peeled off his socks and shoes and carefully set them to one side.

She giggled and fished another French fry from the sack. "This is so much fun. I'm glad we decided to skip the restaurant."

"Uh-huh." Skip the only four-star restaurant in Galveston, skip the birthday cake he'd arranged for the waiter to deliver to their table.

Let it go, Jack. This is what she wants. Spontaneity.

"Open wide." She snuggled closer.

And the next thing he knew they were feeding each other French fries. Her fingertips lightly sweeping his lips. The easy way she touched him sent something hot and urgent gushing through his veins. He tasted salt and potato, but his tongue burned with the indefinable flavor of her skin.

They drank from the root beer together, their heads touching as they simultaneously sucked on the straws. Next, she tackled the shrimp sandwich, moaning with such gusto he couldn't help but wonder what magnificent noises she made in bed.

"Oh, this is so good."

His gaze dropped to her mouth, and he spotted a speck of tartar sauce clinging to her lush bottom lip.

He sat mesmerized by that tiny droplet. Then her tongue darted out and whisked away the object of his fascination.

They sat eating and watching the sunset. After they finished, CeeCee gathered up the wrappers, padded to the trash can a few yards away, weaving through the throng on the seawall. Jack's gaze followed her slender frame. He loved to watch her walk. The way she bounced with so much verve, so much life.

In that moment, a dark thought hit him. Who was he kidding? He could never be right for CeeCee. She needed someone more like Zack. Someone who could match her exuberance.

His heart filled with longing.

How he wanted her!

But was he playing the fool? Acting out of character in a sad attempt to win a woman he could never have?

She returned, smiling in the moonlight. She dropped from the seawall to the sand. "Come on," she invited, reaching a hand to him. "Let's go wading in the surf."

He hesitated. From somewhere down the seawall came the sounds of a band warming up.

Arms outstretched, head thrown back, she

twirled across the sand, her skirt spinning out from her like a glorious red flag. "Come catch me, Wild Man," she dared, then took off down the beach.

Rolling up his pant legs, he then followed her into the water, fighting his natural tendencies, trying his best to be carefree and reckless, just the way she liked.

⁂

ZACK WASN'T ACTING LIKE ZACK TONIGHT.

Gone was his teasing banter, his wolfish grin, his take-no-prisoners charm. He seemed quiet, subdued, contemplative even.

Much more like his brother Jack.

And that bothered CeeCee.

She didn't want to think about Jack. Not tonight. Not this weekend. All she wanted was a scorching affair with Zack. Nothing complicated. Nothing either of them would regret. Just have a damn good time and make lots of great memories.

Because memories were all she would ever have.

She refused to tempt fate, to defy the Jessup family whammy by falling in love. She could never hurt the man she cared about by subjecting him to the curse. So she would collect her memories, remember the day, and not dwell on what she couldn't have.

Jack.

She stopped walking, turned, and saw Zack silhouetted in the moonlight, looking identical to his twin brother.

Uncertainty struck her. Maybe she shouldn't have a fling with him. Maybe, instead of making her feel better about not being able to have Jack, a casual affair with Zack would only make her feel worse.

Especially since Zack showed signs of liking her as much as Jack did. It was all too confusing.

What she needed was something to take her mind off the issue. They needed to do something wild and crazy and unexpected. CeeCee's gaze swept the seawall, searching for a diversion, searching for anything to distract her.

The purple-and-blue neon sign flashed from across the street.

Tattoos.

CeeCee's breath caught. She'd always wanted a little tattoo. Something discreet in a place where most people wouldn't see. Something to remind her that she was a free spirit and loving it. And Zack was the kind of guy game for such adventure. Who knew? He might already have tats. It would be something they could share. A memory to be made.

She ran back up the beach to Zack and jumped into his startled arms. She wrapped her legs around his waist and buried her face against the hollow of his neck. He smelled wonderful.

"Whoa," he said, latching on to her with both hands.

She mussed his hair. He looked into her face, the moonlight accentuating his masculine features.

"What's going on?" he asked.

"Are you up for something really crazy?"

"Er...I don't know. What have you got in mind?"

"Come on, where's the risk-taking maniac your brother is always bragging about? Mountain climbing and hang gliding. Alligator wrestling and bar brawling—

"What's going on in the wicked little mind of yours, CeeCee?"

Heavens above, she loved looking at him. His eyes twinkled at her, and the corners of his lips edged upward. She ran a finger along his cheek, felt his body tense beneath her.

"Just say yes." She slipped from his grasp and dropped to the sand.

"Say yes to what?"

She took his hand and tugged him toward the seawall to retrieve their shoes. "Say yes to yes."

"Okay, okay." He laughed, perching on the edge of

the wall to put his socks and shoes back on. It was a soothing laugh that warmed her to her toes. "Yes."

"Jack?"

"What?" His eyes widened in alarm.

"Oh, I did it again." She slapped a hand across her mouth. "I'm so sorry I keep calling you by Jack's name. But when you laughed just now, you sounded exactly like him."

"It's all right. We're twins. We sound alike."

"Well, tie your shoes and come along then.

"Where to?"

"You'll see."

"Tell me what you're up to, CeeCee," he demanded in a sexy, commanding, masculine way.

"Why, to get inked. No self-respecting motorcycle man and his woman should be without one."

A TATTOO?

Jack balked, digging his heels into the sand. He didn't want a tattoo. He wanted to take CeeCee to supper at the four-star. He wanted to kiss her on the ferry ride. He wanted to whisper sweet nothings to her on the horse-drawn carriage. He wanted to draw a bath, fill it with peach-scented soaps, and slosh around in it with her. He wanted to feed her champagne and chocolate-covered strawberries. He didn't want to eat po'boys from a paper sack or walk the beach barefoot, and he certainly didn't want to get a tattoo.

"Why do you want a tat?"

"Because they're sexy and besides, a tattoo represents freedom."

The woman certainly had skewed ideas of freedom. "How do you figure?"

"The freedom to do what I want, when I want, without anyone telling me no."

"You know what they say about freedom, don't you?"

"No."

"It means you don't have anything to lose."

She got really quiet then, and her face went serious. "Maybe they're right. I don't have anything to lose."

Jack felt awful. He'd inadvertently reminded her of that stupid curse. He wanted to reach out to her, tell her that she *did* have something to lose. Something very precious; her ability to give and receive love.

CeeCee shook off her momentary gloom. "I'm considering a dove on my tushy. Small. Very tasteful. Or maybe a dolphin. What do you think?"

"Honestly? I think there's no need to elaborate on perfection."

"Oh, you!" She tickled him lightly in the ribs. "What are you going to get? A big old Harley on your bicep? Maybe a lion or a tiger? Something ferocious? How about a Tasmanian devil?"

"I was thinking maybe a heart with 'CeeCee' running through it."

She stopped and stared at him. "You're kidding. Right?"

He shrugged. Uh-oh. Had he said something wrong? Cautious as a barefoot man walking on a carpet of glass shards, he studied her.

"Why would you want my name on your arm?" Suddenly she looked panic-stricken and Jack realized his mistake. "You wouldn't want the name of some woman you barely knew for three weeks once upon a time, lingering on your arm forever, would you?"

"Relax. I'm kidding."

"Whew." She laughed shakily. "You certainly had me going there for a minute."

"And you had me going when you said we were getting tattoos."

"I wasn't kidding, though."

Jack looked up and realized they'd been moving steadily to this little parlor across the street from the seawall. The rubber had met the road. He was going to have to get a tattoo or tell CeeCee he wasn't Zack.

But if CeeCee learned his real identity before she made love to him, before she had a chance to fall in love with him, she'd be humming, "Hit the Road, Jack."

That thought was more terrifying than tattoos and not just because his heart would be irreparably damaged, but because CeeCee would never have her happily-ever-after if she keep insisting on chasing after bad boys.

The red neon sign flashed. *Tattoos, Tattoos, Tattoos.*

He took in a deep breath, his gaze sweeping across the grungy building. Did he spill his guts? Or keep his mouth shut?

"CeeCee," he said. "There's something I have to tell you."

"Yes?"

Their eyes met.

"Er... uh..." He scrambled to come up with a good excuse, a way out of this.

She touched his arm, her eyes open, honest, trusting. "What's on your mind, Zack?"

He couldn't do it. He couldn't tell her the truth, couldn't stand to see the disappointment in her eyes.

"Do they take credit cards? 'Cause I'm low on cash." He jerked a thumb at the tattoo parlor/

"It's on me. Come on." She pushed open the door plastered with bumper stickers advertising the shop owner's liberal politics. The bell over the door tinkled.

Like a condemned man headed to the gallows, Zack followed.

Help! How was he going to get out of this? *This'll teach you to try to pull a fast one on the woman you love.*

"Can I help you, dudes?"

The man behind the counter wore a red bandanna wrapped around his forehead, a suede leather vest with fringe on the bottom, no shirt, and faded holey blue jeans. Tattoos covered a good portion of his body, not to mention the numerous body piercings. From earlobes to nose to eyebrows and beyond. His dark hair, threaded with a bit of gray, hung long down his back.

Gulp. *Hello rubber, meet road.*

"We want tattoos," CeeCee chirped.

"Are you sober, dudes?" He narrowed his eyes and studied them.

"As judges." CeeCee smiled.

"'Cause I can't tattoo you if you're drunk."

"We're not drunk," Jack assured him although he was beginning to wish for a tall bottle of Pedro's tequila.

"Sweet. Pick out which ones you want, dudes." The *Big Lebowski* wannabe waved a hand at all four walls covered floor-to-ceiling with thousands of tattoos. "They're arranged in sections. Feminine stuff like butterflies and unicorns are over on the left, the masculine stuff on the right, unisex ones at the back."

CeeCee dragged Jack to the back wall. "Oh, look. You could get a mermaid."

"Nah."

"Stick of dynamite?"

"I don't think so." He made a face.

"A Tweety Bird?"

He shook his head.

"You're right. Too kiddish. We gotta find something that screams Zack! Let's check out the macho section."

Then he saw the caduceus, before he even thought, he reached out a hand to tap the picture. "I'll have this one."

"A caduceus?" She frowned and belatedly he realized his mistake. He was supposed to be Motorcycle

Zack, not Dr. Jack. "Why would you want a caduceus?"

"No, not the caduceus. This one." He let his finger slip to the artwork directly below the caduceus.

A grinning red devil.

Wonderful.

"That suits you to a tee." CeeCee chuckled, then added, "Now come help me pick out mine."

For the next half hour they browsed the shop. But while CeeCee looked at tattoos, Jack looked at CeeCee. His gaze caressed her creamy, flawless skin, and he cringed at the thought of her marring such exquisite beauty with a tattoo.

"You dudes ready?" the Big Lebowski asked when CeeCee finally managed to narrow her selection to a small, tasteful dolphin.

"Yes," CeeCee told him, then whispered to Jack, "I'm going to have it on my tushy."

He visualized her firm little fanny decorated with art and he hardened instantly. Then he realized that Tattoo Dude would get an eyeful of that fanny, too, and he clenched his jaw.

"You sure of your choices?" Tattoo Dude asked. "This stuff don't come off with soap and water."

"We're sure." CeeCee nodded.

"Then sign these waivers." He pushed two clipboards with the appropriate forms and ink pens at them.

"I'm so excited," she whispered to Jack, scrawling her name in her freewheeling, loopy script. "I've dreamed of doing this for years."

Damn, why did she have to be so happy when he was still racking his brain for a way out?

"Thanks so much for doing this with me." She squeezed his hand. "You're the greatest. I wouldn't have had the courage to go through with it without you."

Okay. He could do this. He had survived medical school. If he could survive that grueling schedule, he could survive this. Marking himself for life with the devil's effigy was no biggie. If this was the sacrifice it took to win CeeCee, then he would gladly accept the ink. Anyway, it was chic to decorate one's body with ink art. Lots of people did it. So what if few physicians sported them. He would start a new trend.

"You're so cool." CeeCee squeezed his arm again, and in that moment, Jack felt like the king of the world.

All his life he'd wanted to be thought of as cool and hip and badass, just like Zack, but his cautious nature had prevented him from either following or leading the crowd when it wasn't prudent. Now, he finally had his chance to test his mettle. Did he have what it took to be a wild man?

"Who's up first?" The man gathered up his thick graying hair and pulled it into a ponytail with a rubber band he'd had on his wrist.

Jack glanced at CeeCee. She looked nervous. She worried her bottom lip with her teeth, restlessly shifting her weight from side to side. He didn't think he could stand watching her go through the process. Maybe after he finished, he could talk her out of it.

"I'll go first."

"Where you gonna put it?" the guy asked.

Jack rolled up his left sleeve. "Upper arm."

"Have a seat in the chair."

The tattoo artist gestured toward what looked like a massage chair situated behind the front desk. Swallowing hard, Jack sat.

The tattoo artist plunked down on a four-legged stool, unwrapped a packet of tattoo supplies, and spread them out on a rolling tray. He then flicked on a bright gooseneck lamp and focused it on Jack's upper arm.

"Do you sterilize your equipment?" Jack eyed the needles suspiciously.

"Got my own autoclave, dude."

"Good to know." Jack raised his eyebrows.

"Can I watch?" CeeCee asked.

"Sure, pull up a chair," he offered magnanimously.

CeeCee complied, arranging herself close enough to observe but out of the tattoo artist's light.

"You ready?" he asked Jack.

"As I'll ever be."

The Big Lebowski wannabe turned on the power. His tattoo gun made a buzzing noise.

Cringing, Jack closed his eyes and prayed the electricity would go out or that the guy's tattooing apparatus would short circuit or a spur of the moment hurricane would kick up and blow in across the island to topple the tattoo hut.

He braced himself for the pain.

But it never came.

"Mick!" A woman's voice broke the silence.

Jack's eyes opened to see a very pregnant woman standing in the room, her eyes fixed on the tattoo artist.

"Can't you see I'm busy, Carrie?"

"I'm having contractions, and they're only two minutes apart. You gotta take me to the hospital right now."

Mick turned pale. "Okay, okay, honey." He looked at Jack. "Sorry, dude, my old lady's in labor, the ink'll have to wait."

Jack blew out a sigh of relief. Sometimes prayers really were answered. "No sweat."

Carrie hollered and sank to the floor.

Oh, no!

Mick and Jack jumped up simultaneously and rushed to her side. Her face contorted with pain, and she clutched her abdomen.

"How many pregnancies have you had?" Jack asked, automatically slipping into doctor mode without thinking twice.

"This is my third. Oh gosh, I don't think I'm going to make it to the hospital."

"I'll call 911." CeeCee sprang to the desk.

You can't act like a doctor; you'll give yourself away, the voice that had kept him cautiously assuming Zack's identity for three weeks protested.

Forget that nonsense. Jack had no choice. He *was* a doctor, and he had to help this woman. If he blew his charade, then he blew his charade. Under no circumstances would he risk a patient's well-being.

"Have you ever done Lamaze?" he asked Carrie.

"Uh-huh."

"Great, then start practice your breathing."

She obeyed him, breathing in short panting he-he-he-he's.

He calmed her, and CeeCee joined them on the floor. She checked the mother's pulse while Jack slipped a pillow under her head and spoke soothingly.

Mick paced the tattoo parlor. Carrie had another

contraction and screamed loud enough to raise the roof off the building.

Luckily, the ambulance arrived before Jack ended up having to deliver the baby, and it whisked the woman away. Mick went into the back of the shop where they apparently lived, gathered up his two older children, and followed in the family car.

As a favor to Mick and Carrie, CeeCee and Jack locked up the shop for them and slipped the key under the door when they were finished.

"Wow." CeeCee turned to him.

"Some night, huh?"

She reached out and took his hand. "Let's walk."

They meandered in silence for a while, CeeCee's shoes striking a lazy rhythm against the cement. Jack was dying to know what was going on inside her head. He angled her a couple of surreptitious glances, but he couldn't tell what she was thinking.

"You were great with that mom," CeeCee said at last.

"Thanks."

"You were so calm."

He shrugged casually, but inside he was quaking. Had she figured out he wasn't Zack?

"I mean I'm a physical therapist and even I was flustered."

"You don't see a woman go into labor every day."

"Neither do you."

"True."

"You were as cool and calm and collected as your brother."

"I guess I must have picked up a few tips from Jack. Plus, I've taken first-aid classes. It's important to know first aid and CPR in my line of work."

"You're a multifaceted guy. Much deeper than Jack led me to believe."

She didn't know the half of it.

"We didn't get our tattoos," she went on, "but we did have some excitement."

"Yes. But we're not done yet."

"What do you mean?"

He would show her he could be spontaneous, and it didn't require getting a tattoo or assisting a pregnant woman in labor. Without another word, he leaned over, scooped her into his arms, and carried her down the seawall.

"What are you doing?"

"You want spontaneous. I deliver."

"But your knee," she protested.

"It's fine. I've been healed by the best."

He stalked toward the horse-drawn carriage stand, zigzagging through a throng of curious onlookers.

"Zack, put me down."

She sounded scandalized but looked pleased. Her head was thrown back, exposing her pale neck glimmering in the moonlight. Her hair swished enticingly against his forearm.

"Hush, woman."

"Oh, my," she whispered, her green eyes snapping pure passion.

He hired the carriage and gave the driver the address to their bed-and-breakfast. Settling her onto the seat, he climbed in beside her, then tucked her securely into the curve of his arm.

"Now," he said, "isn't this much more romantic than any tattoo?"

"Yes," she admitted and burrowed against his chest.

Laughing, he kissed her.

❧ 12 ❧

They necked for the entire two-mile ride. Moist mouths joining. Tongues strumming. Eyelashes lowered. Teeth gently nipping.

Shod hooves clomped against cobblestones. The carriage's wooden wheels creaked as they rumbled past restaurants and nightclubs. Muffled strains of Dixieland jazz spilled into the night. The driver clicked his tongue, guiding the horse.

But CeeCee heard nothing except the strong, steady beating of Zack's heart.

A myriad of scents wafted on the breeze. Frying shrimp from the seafood place in the middle of the block. Freshly popped popcorn from a street vendor. Robust garlic, tangy oregano, and zesty onion from Mario's Pizza on the corner.

But CeeCee smelled nothing except Zack's heady, manly aroma.

The well-worn leather seat was smooth against her bottom. Gritty sand filled the soles of her shoes. Her charm bracelet lay cool against her wrist.

But CeeCee felt nothing except Zack's arm held tightly around her waist, and his firm lips pressing against hers with just the right amount of urgency.

The lights around them were bright. Beer signs flickered from O'Hara's Pub. Old-fashioned, turn-of-the-twentieth-century streetlamps lit the way past the regal mansions of a bygone era. Lights twinkled gaily from the tops of buildings as they approached the Strand.

But CeeCee saw nothing except Zack's deep, penetrating dark eyes staring at her in wonderment, as if she were the only woman in the world.

Everything else was peripheral and unimportant. Her focus was narrowed to one thing and one thing only.

Zack Travis.

The driver pulled up outside their inn. Zack paid him, then scooped her into his arms once more, and laughing, carried her up the stoop and into the house.

CeeCee giggled, impressed by his impulsiveness. He was as impetuous as she. Seizing the moment.

Enjoying the present. Not fretting about tomorrow and what the future might or might not bring.

It was the only way to live.

Happiness, she had once heard someone say, was not getting what you wanted, but rather wanting what you got.

And for now she had gotten Zack.

It was enough.

Or so she kept telling herself.

"This way, my lady." He led her up the stairs, her hand tucked firmly in his.

The closer they got to the bedroom door, the louder CeeCee's heart knocked until she feared all the guests in the bed-and-breakfast would hear her. How embarrassing it would be if the inn owners caught her sneaking Zack into her bedroom.

Because she had made up her mind. Tonight, she was going to set a match to this powder keg of sexual attraction that had been smoldering between them for three long weeks. She was not going to back down or run away.

She wanted him.

Desperately.

He stopped outside her bedroom door, took her room key from her, and unlocked it. Then he drew her into his arms. She stared at him, her body trembling.

"May I come inside with you?"

"Do you really have to ask?"

He grinned.

She opened her door with one hand, grabbed him by the collar with the other, and pulled him in after her. She was so busy kissing him and undoing the buttons on his shirt that she smelled the scented candles before she saw them.

Pulling back, she swept her gaze around the room. A dozen candles were strategically placed. The bed had been turned down and rose petals had been strewn across the sheets. On the dresser sat a tray of chocolate-covered strawberries and a bucket of iced champagne.

Zack was busy planting kisses down her neck and softly kneading her buttocks.

"Wait. Stop."

"What is it?" He raised his head and peered at her. His eyes were glassy with passion.

"What's all this?" She swept a hand over the room.

Trepidation flitted through her. Zack had gone to an awful lot of trouble to romance her. Suddenly she found it hard to breathe.

No. No. No. This couldn't be happening. He couldn't like her this much. Last night's filet mignon dinner had been bad enough, but she had accepted his explanation that it was a thank-you for the physical therapy treatments. This setup with the wine and the roses went far beyond thank you.

"Do you like it?" He looked quite pleased with himself.

"You planned this," she said flatly.

"Well, yeah." He blinked, confusion on his face. "I thought you'd be delighted."

"You thought wrong."

"What have I done? I don't understand."

"I told you from the beginning I can't get serious about you. I can't get serious about any man. I just want to have fun, Zack."

"I still don't understand. It's a birthday surprise."

"But you shouldn't have planned anything." Her voice held a desperate note. She had wanted so badly to have a red-hot fling with Zack. Had wanted only a physical relationship with a man who wanted nothing else from her.

"Sweetheart, you're overreacting."

"Jack's the one who plans," she whispered, her voice thick. The truth was deeper than she wanted to admit. Maybe her anxiety sprung from the fact that she was liking Zack too much and not the other way around. "You're supposed to be spontaneous, free-spirited. You should have made love to me on the beach, Zack, not orchestrated this elaborate seduction."

"It doesn't mean anything, CeeCee, I swear. I just thought you'd enjoy it."

"See. That's the problem. You were being thoughtful! You're supposed to be selfish."

"Easy, sweetheart, easy," he soothed. "I promise you're blowing this way out of proportion. I'm still leaving in a week, and you'll probably never see me again."

"Really?" She slanted him a sideways glance.

"Really." He reached out and drew her to him once more.

She felt so conflicted. On the one hand, if she were a normal, non-cursed woman, she would be flattered that he had gone to so much trouble to romance her, but as a hapless casualty of the Jessup family whammy, she was dismayed by his caring, his attention to detail.

What did this mean? That he thought she was special?

CeeCee groaned inwardly. She couldn't be special. Not to Zack. Not to Jack. Not to anybody. She was hexed. Jinxed. Doomed. Any man who looked at her as a long-term love interest would be sorely disillusioned. With Zack, she had believed them both to be safe from heartbreak. Now, she wasn't sure about anything.

And maybe, just maybe, whispered a little voice in the back of her mind, you're afraid the perfect man wouldn't be so perfect if you had him for your very own.

"Let's enjoy the moment, CeeCee, it's all any of us has." He tucked a strand of hair behind her ear. His breath was warm on her skin.

"Promise you're not going to fall in love with me, Zack?"

"Sweetheart, I would promise you the moon to get you tucked under those covers with me."

"Ah," she said. "That's what I want to hear. A selfish man."

CeeCee surrendered to her physical urgings and curled into him, feeling his heat, his hardness. In an instant, his mouth was on hers, giving her another one of his mind-altering, body-shaking kisses. His breathing came in fast, uneven spurts. His hands were all over her at once, but it wasn't enough.

Her insides felt ready to detonate. Her skin seemed too tight, her belly too heavy, her breasts too sensitive.

More. She needed so much more.

She tugged his shirt from his waistband, then slipped her hands up under it and across his bare back. His hands roved over her hips; his mouth never left hers.

It was hot and sexy, and she ached to her very toes for him.

He pulled her to the edge of the bed, and they collapsed down together on the plush roses. The lush scent wafted up to greet them. She luxuriated in the rich, erotic aroma.

And then, without any warning, an image of Jack's wonderful face popped into her head.

Zack was kissing her like there was no tomorrow. His mouth on her cheeks, her eyelids, her chin, her throat, but in a bit, he stopped, pulled back, and looked down at her.

"What's the matter? You stopped responding. Just because I'm a selfish rogue, doesn't mean I don't please my women."

"It's not you," she said, wondering at the wall of tears building in her throat.

He snorted and rolled to one side. "What is it then? You keep claiming you can't have anything but a casual relationship, yet every time things get hot and heavy you slow down. Why?"

"I was just thinking about Jack."

"Again!"

She nodded, miserable that she had upset him, worried why she couldn't stop thinking about Jack.

Here she was having a wild old time, and he was down in Mexico giving of himself to help poor children. She should be ashamed.

"Have you noticed that every time we come close to having sex you bring up Jack's name?"

"No? Yeah?"

"You use him as a barrier between us."

"Do I do that? Really?"

"You tell me."

"I guess I do," she mused.

"Face it, lady, you've got some serious issues with my brother."

"It's not that. I just don't want to hurt him."

Zack reached out and gently stroked her curls. "How would our having sex hurt Jack?"

"He's jealous of your romantic conquests." CeeCee shrugged and turned her head, distracted by Zack's fingers running through her hair. She was aroused enough without him touching her.

"Is he?"

"Surely you knew?"

"And what about you, CeeCee?" He chucked a finger under her chin, tilting her face up to meet his. "This is between you and me. It's got nothing to do with Jack."

"You don't understand."

"So tell me." He draped his legs over hers, holding

her down on the bed beside him.

"It's complicated. I'm not sure I understand it myself."

"Maybe I didn't go to medical school like Jack, but I'm not stupid. Try me. I might see things more clearly than you think."

She raised a hand to push a sheaf of hair from her eyes. The charm bracelet at her wrist jangled.

"I think Jack has a crush on me," she said after a long pause.

"Yeah?" Jack held his breath, then asked, "But you keep saying you don't have sexual feelings for him."

"He's one of my best friends."

"And that's all?"

"Yes," she replied firmly. Then she shook her head. "No."

Jack raised an eyebrow, and his spirits soared. "So what is it? Yes or no?"

"I don't know," she said mournfully and lifted one shoulder in a regretful half shrug.

"If Jack is the one you really want, then why are you here in bed with me?"

"I can't have Jack. I told you about my family curse. You have no idea what it's like, knowing you can't trust any man. That any love affair I'm involved in is doomed to end in failure."

"You don't know that for certain."

"Yes, I do. There's not a man on the face of the earth who can defeat the curse."

"Well, if anyone could, it's Jack. He's very determined, and he doesn't love lightly. In fact, I don't think he's ever really been in love with anything except medicine. Unless he's in love with you. If that's the case, he would fight for you tooth and nail. He's the most loyal guy I've ever known."

It felt weird talking about himself in such glowing terms, but he had to make her see that he *was* different from any man she'd ever known. He wasn't a quitter and he wasn't a coward. He'd do anything for her.

Even go so far as to perpetuate this accidental hoax.

"It's more than the curse," CeeCee admitted in a whisper. "Even if there wasn't a curse, I'd still be too terrified to ever get married."

"And why is that?"

At last! They were getting down to the nitty-gritty and he would find out exactly what scared her so much.

"I wouldn't begin to know how to have a successful marriage. Not a clue. I've only had bad examples. Everything starts out all champagne and roses, and the next thing you know there's shouting and accusations being thrown and men walking out

the door. It's not just the curse. Being lousy at rela-
tionships is my heritage. I don't know anything else."

"Yes, but, CeeCee, you're not your family. You're
an intelligent woman with a lot going for you. You
don't have to repeat toxic patterns."

"But don't you see? I don't know what to replace
those patterns with."

He lay beside her, gently patting her arm, not
knowing what else to say.

She took a deep breath. "And then I keep
thinking about Jack. About how unfair it is that he's
in Mexico working hard, probably not eating right or
getting enough sleep, and here I am this close to
having sex with his twin brother." CeeCee measured
off an inch. "What kind of person does that
make me?"

"Maybe Jack isn't as miserable as you think," he
said, grasping at straws, searching for anything to
make her feel better. "Maybe he wouldn't even mind
if the two of us got together."

Propping herself up on her elbow, she looked him
in the eyes. "I'm not going to lie. I'm very attracted
to you, Zack. But I think it'd be best if you went back
to your own room. The moment's gone, and I don't
think we're going to get it back."

J ack was frantic.

Things weren't working out the way he'd planned. As Zack, he couldn't seem to close the deal with CeeCee. Couldn't get her to have sex with him. Where was he making his mistakes? What could he do differently?

It was Saturday evening. When they'd arrived home from Galveston two hours earlier, CeeCee couldn't seem to get away from him fast enough. He couldn't figure her out. What did she want?

In desperation, he turned to Miss Abercrombie for advice later that evening.

And found himself swallowed up by a bean bag chair in her flashback-to-the-sixties living room. The walls were painted a neon orange. Beaded curtains separated the rooms instead of doors. The couch was a paisley print. A lava lamp, mood ring, and a statuette of the Beatles graced her knickknack shelf. She had Jefferson Airplane on her old record player and was urging him to drink ginseng tea and eat her homemade brownies. Frankly, he was afraid to touch the stuff.

Miss Abercrombie sat on the couch with Muffin perched in her lap. She adjusted her glasses and peered at him. "It's simple, young man."

"It's not simple at all, Miss A. In fact it's very complicated."

She shook her head. "What you know about women, son, could fill a thimble."

"But CeeCee's not like most women."

"Well, I admit her problem is a little unique, but her emotions aren't."

"Throw me a lifeline here. I'm not following you."

"You're going to have to drive her into Zack's arms. She's conflicted. Torn between two men. Before you can convince her to give herself to Zack, she's got to know that Jack's isn't going to be heartbroken by her actions."

He shook his head.

"You've got to make her think Jack is off having as much fun in Mexico as she could be having right here with Zack."

He mulled over what Miss Abercrombie was

saying. It did make sense. If he could set CeeCee's mind at ease about him, then she could let down her guard with Zack.

"Okay, so how do I accomplish that?"

Miss Abercrombie leaned in close, a sassy smile on her elderly face. "Here's what we do."

"CeeCee, darling, I was wondering if you could do me the tiniest favor." Miss Abercrombie and Muffin stood on her doorstep.

"Won't you come in," CeeCee invited, ushering her guests into her living room. "How can I help you?"

Miss Abercrombie stroked Muffin's fluffy head. "I need to speak with young Dr. Jack, and he told me that you knew how to get in touch with him."

"I do have the landline number of the place he's staying, but I think he meant for me to use it only in case of an emergency."

The thought of talking to Jack turned her stomach and she couldn't really say why. She hadn't spoken to him in over seven weeks, and she worried what he would say.

"Well, this isn't exactly an emergency, but it is

important. That obnoxious Missing Link person is claiming my Muffin bit him, and he's suing me."

"Oh, no!"

"Yes. I need Jack to give my lawyer a deposition saying that Muffin did not bite that man."

"Muffin most certainly did not bite him. I was there, too. I'll give the deposition for you."

"That's nice, dear, but I need Jack's statement, too. So could you just call him for me, please?" Dramatically she laid a hand across her chest. "Today, if you please. The sooner I get this cleared up, the better it will be for my poor aging heart."

"Okay. Sure. I'll contact the place where he's staying and leave a message for him to call you."

"That'd be wonderful."

"It might take a while for him to answer, though. He's very busy."

"That's all right." Miss Abercrombie got to her feet. "Ta-ta, dear. Let me know when you hear something."

TWENTY-FIVE MINUTES LATER, JACK STOOD IN MISS Abercrombie's apartment, his cell phone in his hand. He'd just gotten a call from the coordinator at the place where he'd been staying in Mexico that he'd gotten a message from a Miss CeeCee Adams, asking him to call a Miss Abercrombie.

What a mess he was making of things.

"You can't call her back this soon," Miss Abercrombie said. "She thinks you're calling her from a landline at the place where you were working."

"Don't worry. I have a feature that lets me set my number as an out-of-area call no matter where you're calling from," Jack told her.

"I'll trust you on this," Miss Abercrombie said. "I don't know anything about these newfangled electronic gadgets."

Jack paced Miss Abercrombie's living room and repeatedly checked his watch. He couldn't stand much more waiting. "You've got the music ready?"

"Selina's greatest hits." She put the vinyl in question on to play.

"Let's hear your Spanish accent again."

Miss Abercrombie purred some seductive Spanish phrases, adroitly rolling her Rs. "Lucky for you I had several Latin lovers when I was a younger woman."

"Lucky me," he muttered and checked his wristwatch again.

"You're about to crawl out of your skin. Go ahead and call her before you burst wide open."

Jack grabbed the telephone. With trembling fingers he called her.

"Hello."

He almost dropped the receiver at the sound of her voice. He took a deep breath and tried his best to sound casual.

"Hey, CeeCee."

"Jack? Is that you?"

"Uh-huh."

"You sound different."

"Probably because I'm so far away."

"And I haven't talked to you in seven weeks. I'd almost forgotten what your voice sounded like."

"I've been busy."

"It's really great to hear from you."

"You, too."

"I...I've missed you."

His heart skipped at the catch in her voice. He wanted to tell her how much he had missed her, too. He had missed being himself, missed being CeeCee's best friend, missed their intimate conversations about anything and nothing.

Miss Abercrombie stood in front of him mouthing, "Now?"

He shook his head. The plan suddenly seemed very stupid. He didn't care about tricking CeeCee. He just wanted to talk to her, to tell her the truth. That he loved her. Had loved her for many months now. Would love her for the rest of his life.

"Oooh, *señor*, you're *muy muy macho. Por favor,* do that again," Miss Abercrombie moaned in a surprisingly young and sexy voice.

Jack glared at his neighbor and made slashing motions across his throat. *Cut! Cut!*

But Miss Abercrombie was giving the performance of a lifetime, and she wasn't about to let up. She cooed Spanish words of love.

Jack frowned, violently shook his head, and mouthed, "Stop it."

But Miss Abercrombie ignored him. Instead, she tuned up for more, moaning and groaning and putting her face close to the receiver to make sure CeeCee got an earful.

"Er...Jack..." CeeCee's voice raised an octave. "You're not alone, are you?"

Miss Abercrombie kept jabbering in fractured Spanish and wriggling around on the couch with a saucy grin. Jack was ready to throttle her.

"CeeCee, I... It's not what you think."

"Oh," she said quickly. "You don't owe me any kind of explanation. Everyone is entitled to a little R & R. You just have a good time."

"I'm not having a good time," he growled, completely frustrated by the way things were turning out.

"Maybe you should tell that to your lady friend.

Sounds like she's having a ball."

"It's not what you think, Cee."

"Every bachelor is entitled to his er...diversions."

"No. No, I'm not entitled. Listen to me, CeeCee. I've got something to tell you."

Muffin barked, enlivened by her mistress' antics.

"That dog sounds exactly like Miss Abercrombie's Muffin," CeeCee commented.

"Really? Probably the Chihuahua from next door. These walls are pretty thin."

"I've really got to hang up now, Jack," she said with false cheerfulness, but he could hear the pain in her voice. "Could you please call Miss Abercrombie? She needs to talk to you."

"But, CeeCee..."

"Gotta go," she said and hung up on him.

He sat staring at the phone. He'd certainly upset her and he felt horrible about it. But wasn't that what he wanted? To upset her enough to send her flying into Zack's arms?

"So?" Miss Abercrombie asked, grinning brightly. "Did she fall for it?"

"She fell all right."

"Then why do you look so sad?"

"Because I just hurt my very best friend in the whole entire world."

WHY ARE YOU CRYING? YOU'VE GOT NOTHING TO CRY about. So Jack has a woman down in Mexico. So what? You should be happy for him, you selfish woman.

She should be happy but instead she was more miserable than the time when she was ten and had eaten fifteen green apples on a dare from one of her stepbrothers. Come to think of it, her mother had thrown out stepfather number two over that belly-ache incident.

The truth is, she was shattered.

Last night in Galveston, Zack had come very close to convincing her that Jack was different from most men. She'd found out the hard way that he was not. He had feet of clay just like the rest of them.

Why was she so disappointed? She'd told Jack they could never be more than friends. It was pure selfishness on her part to think he shouldn't get on with his life.

"I do want him to get on with his life," she argued out loud, staring glumly at her bedroom wall. "I wanted him to find someone to love. Just not so soon."

Liar, you want him to love you.

The thought sprang unbidden from the ether.

She clasped her pillow to her chest and curled into a fetal position, tears still dampening her cheeks.

"No," she whispered. "It's not true. I don't want him to love me. I would only hurt him."

Besides, there was her confounded attraction to Zack. What did that mean?

The doorbell pealed.

"Go away," CeeCee mumbled.

It rang again.

She didn't want company, but she wasn't the type to let the doorbell go unanswered.

Sighing, she sat up and ran a hand through her tangled curls. "Coming, coming," she called out. "Rein in them horses, cowboy."

She padded to the door in her pajamas, threw it open, and found Zack leaning nonchalantly against the jamb.

He looked delicious and more than a little lawless in black jeans, a black Harley muscle shirt, and black boots. His hair was pulled back in a tiny ponytail. She suddenly wondered why she hadn't made love to him at the bed-and-breakfast last night. Some misguided sense of responsibility to Jack.

What had she been thinking? Jack had gotten on with his life; she should be getting on with hers.

"I'm through playing around, CeeCee," Zack said gruffly.

"Wh...what?"

"I've given it time. I've been understanding, but the truth is, I can't wait anymore. I want you. Here. Now. This minute. Say yes, CeeCee," he pleaded. "Say yes."

Her knees turned to peanut butter.

"If you're not interested, or if you can't get over Jack, then tell me and I'll walk away. I'll leave town. I'll leave you alone. I'll..."

Before he could finish his sentence, she grabbed him by the front of his shirt, pulled him into her apartment, and slammed the door closed behind them. She wrapped her arms around his neck, tugged his mouth down to hers, and told herself, *this is all I can have. Jack is not only off-limits; he's found someone else. Zack is here and he wants you. You want him. That's all there is to it and it is enough.*

Zack responded with a passion to equal her own. He scrunched her curls in his hand. His gaze burned into hers. He molded his mouth on hers, kissing her like a brand. He tasted incredible. Tart yet sweet, exotic and fresh and startlingly real. She feasted on him, a most sumptuous buffet.

He pulled away a moment, breathing heavily. "I don't want you to have regrets."

"I won't."

"No turning back this time," Zack said hoarsely.

"Take me as I am, CeeCee, for what I can give you right now."

"Just hush and kiss me again."

This was exactly what she wanted. Heat and passion, no promises of undying love, no whispers of forever. Just Zack, hard and hot and filled with masculine energy.

Then he took her into his arms and carried her into the bedroom. CeeCee did not protest. She let herself go, falling into the steamy vortex that had been drawing at her from the moment she'd met Zack. The sexual chemistry between them was undeniable and anything beyond that did not matter.

He laid her down carefully on the mattress, then stood back to admire her. CeeCee raised a hand to her chest, embarrassed by her comfy but faded pajamas and fluffy pink house slippers.

"Sorry I'm not dressed for the occasion," she apologized, kicking off the slippers.

"You couldn't be sexier in black lace and garters, babe."

"I had no idea shabby pj's were a turn-on," she whispered.

"Oh, yeah. Holey underwear, baggy sweatsuits, anything or nothing. You could make a hospital gown look like designer duds."

She felt herself blush at his compliment. He made

her feel beautiful and special, even if she knew deep down it was only a line. Guys like Zack instinctively knew how to charm. But that was okay with CeeCee. She would take what she could have.

He settled himself beside her, slipped one arm underneath her, then gently kissed her forehead.

He reached for the top button on her shirt, and she realized in surprise that the womanizing Wild Man's hands were trembling. When he undid the last button to reveal her breasts, his breath caught in his lungs with an audible gasp.

"Fair's fair," she said gruffly, touched by the admiration in his eyes. "Off with your shirt as well."

She reached over, pulled his shirt from his waistband, and rolled the soft cottony material up to his chest. Swiftly, he jerked the shirt over his head and tossed it to the floor.

For a moment she simply stared in wonder at that firm, muscled chest, those chiseled biceps. This was all about sexual pleasure, and she drank in the sight of him.

He crooked a devilish grin that sent an icy hot shaft of longing through her heart, and he slid her top off her shoulders.

And things just got better and better from there.

❦ 14 ❧

CeeCee was absolutely incredible. Far more compelling than his most fantastic dreams.

She gave a soft little moan as Jack cupped her breasts and teased her nipples with his thumbs. They grew rock-hard under his caress, delighting him. It delighted him even more when she raised her head and met his mouth.

She inhaled in erotic little gasps, a combination of surprise and arousal. She flowed like the athlete she was, all grace and coordination and strength. Her tongue dueled with his. Her teeth nipped his bottom lip. He could barely hang on to his control. It took his entire concentration not to take her that very second.

Not yet. This was important. Their lovemaking

had to be perfect. And he knew it would be. For he loved her more deeply than he'd ever known it was possible to love another human being.

The hungry way she kissed him only solidified his resolve to take things slowly. They had all night. He would torture her the way she was tormenting him with that wicked tongue of hers, the lusty vixen —relentlessly.

He helped her wriggle out of her pajama bottoms and revised his previous thoughts. At this rate he wouldn't last two minutes.

And that wouldn't do. After all, he had Zack's reputation to uphold.

From his point of view, she was the quintessential woman. Perfect breasts, firm and high, the size of late-summer peaches. Her stomach was flat with the tiniest curve at the apex above her thighs. Her waist was slender, her hips shapely. And those legs! She put all pinup queens ever to decorate a GI's locker to shame.

Jack was a doctor, yes, but he'd never seen an anatomy like this one and to think she was his at long last.

Lovingly, he trailed a hand down her body, lingering at every trigger point that caused her to writhe with pleasure.

"Enough," she whispered huskily, her eyes burning as brightly as if she had a fever. "My turn."

She reached for his waistband. Jack gulped at her boldness, but then again, that was his CeeCee. She never held back from a challenge. She met life head-on.

Her breath still came in heavy, heated spurts, but she did not let that deter her. He leaned back against the pillows, enjoying the moment, relishing her desire.

Unsnapping the button of his jeans, she then went for the zipper, easing it down inch by inch. Occasionally she glanced over at him, flicked out her tongue, and sent him a naughty grin. Raising his hips, he helped her shuck his pants free and toss them in the corner.

He was reminded of the night he returned from Mexico, the night he'd inadvertently started this whole deception.

For a brief second, his passion began to dissipate as he thought about what he was doing. Making love to her under false pretenses. It wasn't the honest thing to do and for his entire life Jack had been the honest, reliable twin.

But as his doubts reared up in his conscience, CeeCee went to work on him with her tongue, strumming it back and forth against one of his nipples, jettisoning him straight into outer space.

He was wearing the briefest of briefs, CeeCee noted. More leopard print. Tarzan in all his manliness.

And there was no hiding his arousal, barely covered by the thin material.

Oh my! The room was hotter than a sauna and twice as steamy.

She kissed him everywhere. His chest, his arms, his legs. He groaned and flailed and twisted his fingers through her hair.

"C'mere, Red," he gasped and hauled her to his chest and things got really real from there.

HE KISSED HER SWEETLY, THEN DEEPLY, AND finally ravenously. CeeCee melted into him. Spun dizzily into a place she'd never been before. Hung there like a kite in the wind. How she wanted this to go on and on and on forever.

If she and Zack could just stay in bed, maybe they could thwart the Jessup family whammy. Maybe the curse only worked when you were out of bed.

What a fantasy. What a dream.

"Focus on me," he said as if reading her mind. "On us. On now. Forget about everything else."

And so she let go of all conscious thought, simply let her body experience what the night held in store.

"I gotta have you," she whispered into his ear. Jack's name was on the tip of her tongue, but at the last minute she managed to bite it back. She wasn't going to make that mistake again. She was with Zack, the temporary twin who made her blood race but that was all.

"I gotta have you, too, babe."

"I can't take it anymore."

"Me, either."

He whisked off his briefs, and they disappeared over the edge of the bed.

Holy Tarzan!

She had no idea he was so...so...magnificently endowed. Now she knew why he had such a reputation with the ladies.

He laughed at her expression. "Surprised? Pleased? Perplexed?"

"*Yikes.*"

He nuzzled her neck. "Don't worry, I'll be gentle."

She felt his heart pounding through his chest, matching the rhythm of her own erratic heartbeat. They pressed their palms together and stared into each other's eyes. He kissed her again, his fingers dancing over her back, causing her to melt.

"Protection?" she whispered.

"Got it covered." He laughed. "Pun intended."

His sheathed hardness throbbed against her thigh, pressing into her soft flesh. A searing moisture flowed through her. She felt on fire, alive with yearning to be one with him. He cuddled her into him, and she arched her hips.

Fever swept her body, clouded her brain. There was no reasoning, no rational thought left. She acted on pure instinct. She lifted her legs and curled them around his waist.

"Come to me," she murmured.

With a groan he surged forward. Her body filled to overflowing with him.

"CeeCee," he cried and to her shock she saw a single tear glisten on his cheek. She reached out and brushed it away with her fingertips. Their lovemaking had moved him to tears? It seemed so out of character for cocky Zack.

He moved deeper into her, taking it slowly at first then upping the tempo. Stroke after stroke, building the fire, escalating the sweet torture.

She clutched his shoulders, begged him for more.

He complied, bringing her to the edge of oblivion.

Her head reeled. Her stomach contracted. She'd

never experienced such physical intensity. Two weeks of sexual teasing had taken its toll.

She hung suspended, staring up at him. At his dark eyes, the curve of his cheek, his scruffy beard. She stared at the face that looked so much like her dear Jack's but wasn't.

Why couldn't he be Jack?

A stabbing loneliness knifed through her at what she could never have, at what she had lost through no fault of her own.

In that awful moment, just before she exploded with an earth-shattering release, she realized she'd just had sex with one twin when she was in love with his brother.

JACK STARED AT THE CEILING. CEECEE WAS CURLED in a ball on the bed beside him sleeping soundly, her legs entangled with his under the sheet. Her hair spread out across his pillow.

His deepest dreams had finally come true.

Part of him was happy, euphoric.

Another part was filled with impending doom.

He'd finally made love to CeeCee, and it had been every bit as wonderful as he'd imagined.

But he had made love to her in the guise of his

twin brother and that wasn't right, even though he had been forced to pose as Zack because her belief in the curse left him no option. His plan, which had once seemed so foolproof, now seemed very foolhardy. What if the whole thing blew up in his face? What if she ended up falling in love with Zack and not him? What if she ended up hating him for his duplicity?

His gut wrenched.

What if he lost not only his lover but his best friend as well?

Jack drew in a deep breath. It was time to tell her the truth. But how? And when? And where?

Closing his eyes, he remembered the intimacy they'd shared. Three times in fact. Even now, just thinking about making love to her had his body responding in a very unruly manner.

She'd been perfect in every way. Her sexual hunger matched his own. She'd known exactly where to touch, exactly what to do to send him spiraling into the stratosphere. She was without a doubt the best lover he'd ever had, not that he had anywhere near Zack's level of experience.

He could only hope and pray he hadn't screwed things up. That she'd forgive him for his charade.

Gulping, Jack opened his eyes and looked over at her. The covers rode low, exposing her silky bare skin.

In repose her normally animated face was calm and serene. She looked like an angel.

His heart flapped raggedly against his rib cage.

"I never meant to hurt you, angel," he whispered. "I just didn't know any other way to get you into my arms."

Should he wake her now and tell her what he must? He reached out a hand to stroke his fingers through her curls. No. Not yet. He had to find the right time, the right place. He had to make certain she'd fallen in love with him first.

HER CELL PHONE WAS RINGING.

Groggily CeeCee reached for the phone on the bedside stand.

"Hello," she muttered. She heard nothing on the other end, but the phone kept ringing.

Huh? She dragged herself to a sitting position, then looked over and saw a man-size lump in her bed. Her pulse skittered like a lizard up a brick wall as it all came back to her.

She'd made love to Zack last night after finding out Jack had another woman.

She froze.

The phone rang again.

Leaning over the edge of the bed, she searched for the insistent sound.

Hmm, Zack's pants were ringing.

"Zack," she said, nudging him with her toe. "You've got a call."

Zack was sound asleep, not moving a muscle.

She poked him again. Nothing. Just like his brother. At the hospital, Jack was notorious for being difficult to awaken when he got a chance to nap on his thirty-six-hour shifts. Apparently, the Travis twins could sleep through a bomb.

The phone chirped a fourth time. Maybe she should just let it go to voice mail.

Fifth ring.

What if it was an emergency?

"Okay, okay, I'll answer it." CeeCee leaned over the bed, hooked Zack's pants with a finger, and hauled them onto the covers with her. She grappled in the pockets, finally found the cell phone, and hit "accept" even though she didn't recognize the number.

"Hello."

"Why, hello," purred a smooth, male drawl that sounded a lot like Zack's. "My, what a sexy voice you have."

"Please don't tell me this is an obscene phone call." CeeCee rolled her eyes to the ceiling.

"No, no, not at all. I'm just not accustomed to a woman answering my brother's phone. Then again, maybe I have a wrong number."

His brother? CeeCee frowned. What was this guy talking about? He wasn't Jack and she was sleeping with Zack and they didn't have any other brothers that she knew about. Surely, it was a wrong number.

"Who's your brother?" she asked.

"Jack Travis. He called and left a message on my machine on Thursday telling me not to worry about showing up for the bachelor auction, but I just now got home. I had a spill on my bike. Nothing major, a slight concussion, but they kept me in the hospital for observation. His message was kind of garbled, and I'm not sure I understood. I thought he was in Mexico."

"Wait a minute. Hold on. I'm confused. Is this Zack?"

"Wild Man Zack Travis Motocross Champion two years in a row," he said proudly.

"Excuse me?" Stunned, CeeCee stared at the man beside her.

If this was Zack on the other end of the telephone, then who in the heck was in her bed!

Who had she made love to last night like a crazed nymph?

"Indeed. Guess what? I had no idea Jack had

returned from Mexico," she said. "In fact, I thought you were staying at Jack's place and that you'd already appeared in the auction on Friday afternoon."

"What? I'm not following you." Then from the other end of the line she heard him say, "Aha. I get it. Jack's been running the old switcheroo on you."

"Come again?" She gritted her teeth and clenched one hand into a fist, barely keeping her anger in check.

Anger that sprang from hurt. She felt confused, betrayed, and duped. How could she have been so gullible? All along it had been Jack she'd given therapy to in the hot tub. Jack that she'd kissed. Jack that she'd just spent the night with.

But if that was the case then who was the *señorita* on the phone last night? And the anonymous Chihuahua?

In an instant, she knew the answer. Miss Abercrombie and Muffin. The Missing Link wasn't suing the elderly lady. She and Muffin were in on Jack's scheme.

"Aw, when we were kids, we used to switch places," the real Zack told her. "When I had a test I couldn't pass, Jack would take it for me. When he had a woman he wanted to ask out, I would do it for him. It's kinda underhanded, but most identical twins pull that sort of thing at least a few times growing up."

"Really," she said dryly.

"But I was always the instigator of the switch," Zack said. "I can't believe Jack pulled this on his own."

"Well," CeeCee said, trying to be fair despite having the strongest urge to kick Jack out of bed. "To his credit, I was the one who assumed he was you, but he went along with it."

"He must really care about you," Zack mused.

"How do you figure?"

"Jack's as honest as the day is long. He'd never pretend to be me in order to win a woman unless he thought he had absolutely no chance on his own."

"How did he think he was going to get away with this?" CeeCee sighed, exasperated now.

Zack was right. She would never have gone to bed with Jack. He was her best friend, and she would have done anything to avoid hurting him. She was shocked by what he'd done. Shocked and guiltily pleased to discover that he had cared enough to pull such a stunt.

Still, no matter his motivation, the bottom line was they were both going to be hurt.

Looking over at him, she shook her head. *Oh, Jack, what have you done?*

"Would you like to know an underhanded way to

wring a confession out of him?" Zack asked, a chuckle in his voice.

"Yes," she said without hesitation.

"Then listen up. I've got a plan that'll take the starch out of Jack's socks and get you the answers you need. We'll teach that son of gun to try the old switcheroo with you."

"Wake up, Zack, we're going skydiving."

"Huh?" Jack blinked at CeeCee.

She was standing over him dressed in a denim jumpsuit and knee-length black leather boots, looking all the world like a dominatrix. Give her a few props, like a whip and handcuffs and she'd be set.

"Remember when you told me that you've always wanted to go skydiving? Well, surprise! I've already called the local parachuting operation, and they've got a class starting in an hour. If the weather's right, we can jump this afternoon."

"But my knee." Jack looked panicky and grabbed hold of his knee. The thought of skydiving terrified him.

"Up, up, up." She whipped the covers off him.

What in the world had gotten into CeeCee? She seemed a woman possessed, tugging on his arm with a determined thrust to her chin and a scary gleam in her eyes.

"Your knee is healed and with your athletic skills, I'm sure you won't have a bit of trouble landing smoothly," she said glibly, and he thought, a little heartlessly. "Now get up and get dressed."

He tried to come up with another excuse, but CeeCee didn't give him time.

She clapped her hands. "Chop, chop. Get moving. The sky awaits."

What was he going to do?

Why, turn on the old Zack charm and lure her back to bed. He gave her a seductive wink, purposely ran a hand across his bare chest, and flicked his tongue over his bottom lip.

"Hey, babe, you look good enough to eat. C'mere." He reached out to grab her wrist, but she danced away.

"What's the matter, Zack? I thought you were the Wild Man," she taunted. "Nothing you won't try. Isn't that right?"

Her angry tone confused him. What was she mad about? Had he done something wrong last night? Had she been disappointed in the sex?

"Uh...that's right."

Just tell her the truth, Jack. Confess you're not Zack. You're terrified of heights and you can't go jumping out of airplanes.

But was now the right time? Especially when she was acting so weird? What had happened to her? He'd expected them to cuddle in bed until noon, then go out for lunch in a nice quiet restaurant. He'd wanted handholding and stolen kisses and deep passionate sighs. He had expected her to fall in love with him.

Instead, CeeCee was revved on superspeed, talking quickly with a hard inflection on the last word of her sentences. She barked out orders like a senior surgeon heading a dicey operation. She drilled him with looks that would make the bravest medical student quake.

Was she always like this after sex? No wonder her other boyfriends never hung around. Her irrational fear of the Jessup family whammy ran deeper than he had imagined.

"Why don't you call and cancel the lesson." He tried soothing her. He gave her what he hoped was an endearing grin and patted the mattress. "So we can spend the rest of the morning in bed. We can go skydiving another day."

"Need I remind you," she said. "Jack will be coming home next week, and you'll be leaving town.

We'll probably never see each other again. Come on, Wild Man, get out of bed. The time has come to put your money where your mouth is and prove you're as daring as everyone claims."

"Last night wasn't proof enough?"

"Sex doesn't count as fearless."

"It does with you." He wriggled his eyebrows suggestively.

"I'm beginning to have my doubts about your supposed fearlessness. Maybe we should change your name from Wild Man to Child Man."

"CeeCee," he protested.

"I'll wait for you in the car." She turned on her heel and walked to the door, then stopped, red hair tumbling down her shoulders, and looked at him with an expression that threatened to stop his heart. "Don't disappoint me, Zack."

THE PLANE VIBRATED WITH SOUND. WAS THE damned thing supposed to be so noisy? And did it have to be so old? He could have sworn the plane was manufactured during World War II. His fear of heights was chomping on him like T-cells on a virus.

Jack huddled beside CeeCee, parachutes harnessed to their backs. They'd spent the last six hours in ground school training, learning far more than he'd ever wanted to know about skydiving.

He'd tried several times to find a way to tell her he wasn't Zack, but they'd been surrounded by instructors and other students all day and the opportunity had never arisen.

And then there was that part of him that whispered that he *could* be like his twin brother. Maybe he could jump out of the plane. If he could ignore the giant boulder in his throat that is. If he could unglue his butt from the seat.

Chicken.

Maybe this was exactly what he needed to prove to himself that he was brave and strong and tough and that his fear of losing her was much greater than his fear of heights.

Then again, maybe he needed a straitjacket and a heavy-duty antipsychotic. They were going to shove him out of a plane and into the empty atmosphere, for pity's sake. Had he lost his everloving marbles?

He looked over at CeeCee. She met his gaze with a stony stare. She'd been like that all day. Edgy, fierce. He still couldn't figure out where he'd gone wrong. Instead of their lovemaking binding CeeCee to him as he'd imagined it would, their passionate night together seemed to have agitated her and pushed them farther apart. His plan was unraveling like a ball of yarn in a roomful of kittens.

The plane climbed higher.

His stomach roiled. Good thing he'd passed on lunch.

Aw, hell. What was he going to do? He couldn't parachute from the plane. He was supposed to be fearless Wild Man Zack. The guy who would try anything once.

He couldn't even handle this tandem jump with the burly ex-paratrooper jump master whimsically called Tiny, sitting calmly on the bench across from them. Beside Tiny sat the other jump master, his exact physical opposite, a fidgety string bean of a man called Moose. Whomever nicknamed these guys had a wry sense of humor.

And he wasn't fearless Zack. He was terrified-of-heights Jack. He had been acrophobic since Zack pushed him out of the chinaberry tree in their back-yard when they were nine years old and he'd broken his collarbone.

Nothing but nothing could possess Jack to free fall out into the wide blue yonder, hurtling one hundred and ten miles an hour to the ground below. He blanched at the mere notion.

Nothing that is, except CeeCee.

He had to do this. For her.

If he jumped, it that would prove to her that if he could let go of his fears and change, then so could she. Nothing less dramatic would work.

In that moment, he knew he was going to have to jump. No lucky weaseling out of it like at the tattoo hut. Not even divine intervention could stop him from his mission.

He tapped his foot restlessly against the floor. Okay, so he wasn't tapping it restlessly. His leg muscles were jumping beyond his control. He couldn't have stopped his knee from bobbing up and down like a jackhammer any more than he could've stop breathing.

"Getting excited?" CeeCee asked, eyebrows raised.

"Yep." It was all the conversation he could manage.

❧

CeeCee's heart thudded. Inside she felt as trembly as Jack's knee. She was surprised he'd let things go this far. Zack had assured her he would back out long before they got to the airplane. She was more than a little apprehensive about skydiving herself. But if he could keep playing his ridiculous game, then so could she.

Who would cry "uncle" first?

She had endured six hours of ground school simply to see how far he would take his masquerade before admitting he really wasn't Zack. Apparently, he was taking it to the limit. When was he going to own up to the fact that he would rather be sealed in a locked cellar with a hundred rats than challenge his fear of heights? Why didn't he just come clean? He was stubborn as a mule.

But she was stubborn, too.

Stubborn and mad and hurt. Did he realize exactly how much he'd wounded her? He'd been the only man in the world she had trusted completely, and he had shattered that trust by lying to her.

And for three weeks!

Her heart ached. Plus, he'd tricked her into making love to him. *Oh, Jack, why?*

Was it because he realized she would never have gone to bed with him if she had known he wasn't Zack? Had she forced his hand? Was she actually in some ways responsible for his deception? And she remembered, he'd never actually told her he *was* Zack on the night of her pool party. She'd simply assumed it and he hadn't corrected her.

Or was it more than that? Had she simply *wanted* to believe in Jack's flimsy ruse?

Still, it was no excuse. He could have corrected her.

"Eleven thousand feet," the pilot announced. "We're over the drop zone."

CeeCee rested a hand on his overactive knee. "This is it, Zack." She placed extra emphasis on his name.

"CeeCee, I..."

Her stomach squeezed and she looked deeply into his dark eyes. Was he about to tell the truth? "Yes?"

"You first," Tiny, the jump master who looked not unlike Dwayne (the Rock) Johnson flicked a finger at Jack. Tiny got to his feet, ducking his head in the cramped confines, and opened the side hatch. Moose went to stand beside him.

Cold air blasted into the cabin. The hair poking out from CeeCee's helmet whipped around her neck. Even in that macho gear she looked impossibly feminine and beautiful.

He felt like a World War II soldier leaving his woman at the train station while heading out on a suicide mission.

"Are you ready?" Tiny asked.

According to their ground school instructor, Jack was supposed to respond with an enthusiastic "Yes!"

He leaned forward, stared out the door at the blue sky and clouds and the tiny scenery far, far below and swallowed hard. His knee bobbed with the rigor of a hound dog scratching an ear with a back leg. "No."

"No?" Tiny blinked.

"I've got something to say to her first." Jack stared at CeeCee and mentally begged her to understand.

Her eyes were on his face, her hands clenched in her lap. "What is it?" she asked.

He met her gaze and held it firm, sweat slicked his palms.

"I'm Jack," he said simply.

"I know." She clenched her jaw.

He saw the muscles work beneath her skin and he felt hopeless.

"You've been pulling the old switcheroo."

"You knew?" Dread seized him and refused to let go.

Silently she nodded, her green eyes filled with so much hurt his gut lurched. To think he'd put that expression on her dear, sweet face. He was a royal bastard.

"But how?" he asked. "Since when?"

"Since this morning. Zack called your cell phone while you were still sleeping."

Ah. So his brother was the impetus behind the impromptu skydiving expedition. He might have known. He felt lower than a snake's belly. It wasn't supposed to turn out like this. The last thing he'd ever wanted was to disillusion her like the other men in her life.

"I can explain," he began.

"I don't want an explanation."

"I did it for you."

"Ha!"

"I did it for *us.*"

"There is no us," she said flatly. "Not anymore. Friends don't lie to each other."

"You've got to listen to me, CeeCee."

"Save your breath. I don't want to hear it. You're just like every other man I've ever known, Jack. I'm not going to feel the least bit badly if you get your heart bruised over this. I tried to warn you."

"You're wrong. I'm not like the others."

She fingered her charm bracelet and frowned. "No. You're not like all these guys. You're worse. At least with them I knew where I stood. I never believed in them. Never put my trust in them."

"I just wanted to prove to you that you could fall in love."

"Oh, Jack, I already knew I could fall in love with you. Why do you think I told you we could never be more than friends? I knew it wouldn't take much to push me over the edge, and now you've gone and ruined everything."

"You're in love with me?" He stared. Had he heard correctly?

She shook her head. "How can I love you? I don't even know who you are anymore. I was afraid I might be falling in love with Zack except I couldn't stop thinking about you. I was so confused. But either way, it doesn't matter. Even if I am in love with you, I can't marry you. There can be no happily ever after for me. Didn't I make that clear enough? Love's got nothing to do with it. I'm cursed, dammit, don't you get it?"

"You're just afraid," Jack said quietly. "Afraid that maybe you aren't cursed, and you'll have to assume responsibility for your own happiness. Afraid you'll no longer have something to blame for your romantic failures."

"You're nuts."

"Am I? You're as afraid of marriage as I am of heights. Admit it."

"Okay. All right. Yes. I'm afraid."

"What's going on here?" Tiny, asked, clearly irritated with them. "Are you two goin' to jump or make love or what?"

Moose just loomed tall and skinny like a silent lodgepole pine.

"Should I kill the engine?" the pilot asked over his shoulder. "Are they jumping?"

"No," CeeCee said at the same time Jack said, "Yes."

The pilot shut off the engine. The silence was almost deafening. Only the sound of their breathing filled the small plane. Jack scooted to the open portal.

"What are you doing?" she shrieked.

"I'm ready to face my fears, sweetheart. I'm trying to prove that there's nothing in this world I wouldn't do for you. Even jump from a perfectly good airplane if that's what it takes."

"Get back over here, Jack, you're not jumping."

"I love you, CeeCee. I want you. For now and always. Curse or no curse. Can't you understand that?"

"Jack, no, please don't do this. I never meant for you to skydive. It was just a ploy Zack and I cooked up to get you to confess. We never thought you'd go through with it."

"It was an effective plan." He reached out and took hold of the strut as he'd been taught.

"You're still going?"

"I can't prove anything to you from inside this plane."

"But what about your knee?"

He shrugged. "I'm ready to accept the consequences of my love. Are you?"

"Are you ready?" Tiny boomed.

"Yes!" Jack shouted.

"Please don't do it," CeeCee cried and reached out to him.

But it was too late.

He'd already jumped.

❧ 16 ❧

Jack loved her.

Of that she had no doubt. Who could overlook such a grand gesture? He'd faced his greatest fear by leaping from a plane eleven thousand feet in the air just to prove to her how much he cared.

The least she could do was follow suit.

"Dammit, he didn't wait for me," Moose finally spoke. "He could get hurt." Then Moose bailed headlong from the plane after Jack.

"Oh my gosh." CeeCee's hand went to her throat. "Is he going to be okay?"

"He'll be fine. Moose is the best." Tiny crooked a beckoning finger at her. "You're next."

CeeCee inched toward the door. She peeked out and saw Jack falling like a stone, Moose right behind.

Terror struck her heart. If anything happened to him, it was all her fault.

What had she done?

At that moment, Jack's parachute opened. Thank God.

"Are you ready?" Tiny shouted to her. "To take a gamble on the most incredible experience of your life?"

Tiny was talking about skydiving, but that wasn't why CeeCee answered, "Yes!"

At Tiny's signal, she climbed out onto the strut, held on with all her might in the eighty-mile-per-hour wind. Her pulse was racing as fast as it had the night before when she and Jack had made love. Memories of the previous night danced in her head, mingled with the adrenaline spiking through her veins. She thought of Jack. Of how he'd shown her with tender kisses, gentle caresses, and soft hugs just how much she meant to him.

"Check in," Tiny called, snapping her back to the present.

She performed the maneuvers she'd been taught, then she let go of the strut and started her free fall.

Tiny followed behind her. Once he was in the air beside her, he tapped on his altimeter to remind her to watch her altitude.

Ten thousand feet.

Good thing Tiny was there. She was so terrified she could barely get her body in the correct position, arching her back, putting her arms and legs out, spread-eagle.

Nine thousand feet.

Falling, falling, hurtling toward the ground at an incredible speed. The fear was intense. She forced herself to smile, to give Tiny a thumbs-up.

Eight thousand.

What if her chute didn't open? Dear God, what if she was killed before she had a chance to tell Jack that she loved him? That she forgave him. Everything passed in a blinding rush.

Seven thousand feet.

Nothing was more important than Jack. Nothing.

Five thousand.

She pulled the cord on her chute. It billowed out in a puffy orange rectangle, slowing her descent.

Once the fear of her chute not opening passed, her adventuresome nature roared to life and she began to enjoy the experience.

Floating suspended. Tranquil. Other than the flapping of her chute in the wind, she heard only silence.

A deep, thoughtful silence.

She'd leaped into the arms of emptiness, trusting

that the parachute would open, trusting she would be okay. Why did she have the courage to do something most people would never dream of doing but she didn't have the courage to do something that almost everyone did—fall in love and get married? Why couldn't she let herself jump into love with Jack? Why couldn't she trust that together, they could break the curse?

Down, down, down she drifted, while her spirit soared at the possibilities. Maybe Jack had been right all along. Maybe the Jessup family whammy was nothing more than self-fulfilling prophecy.

Did she dare hope?

She hit the ground in a landing so softly a two-year-old could have made it. Grinning, she spun around, looking for Jack. Where was he?

She took a deep breath and spied Tiny. He trotted over and gave her a high five. "Great jump."

"Thanks." She felt her face flush with happiness, but she didn't care about what she had accomplished. She just wanted to see Jack and make sure that he was all right. Stripping off her helmet, she then tucked it under her arm.

They were in a large open field, no one else around. She had to find him. Had to tell him what revelations had occurred to her up there in the air.

She had to tell him that she loved him. That she

forgave him his deception. That she understood why he'd pretended to be his twin brother.

For he was right. She would never have allowed herself to get intimate with Jack. He'd done what he had to do to achieve his goal, and she could not fault him for that.

Jack was nothing if not determined.

But where was he?

She started to panic and turned to Tiny. "Where's my friend?" she asked. *My friend, my lover, my mate, my everything.* "Did you see where he came down?"

"Isn't that him right over there?" Tiny pointed and she saw a Drop Zone van parked on the side of the road, with Jack and Moose leaning nonchalantly against the hood.

She ran to Jack, laughing and crying and breathing hard. "Hi."

"Hey, you," he said, catching her as she hurled herself headlong into his arms.

Jack pulled her to his chest, gazing at her with a sultry expression that was pure bad boy. A look that told her he was remembering last night and hoping for many more such nights to come. Good thing he was holding her tight because her legs were so rubbery that she would have slid straight to the ground.

"What did you think of the dive?"

"It was wonderful, exhilarating, terrifying, fabulous, fantastic," she enthused, then lowered her voice. "It changed my life."

"Mine, too," he whispered and pressed his lips to the top of her head. "I'm so glad we did it together."

"You jumped out of an airplane for me."

"Sweetheart, that isn't the half of it. I would walk across hot coals for you; I'd swim with sharks. I would even get a tattoo, and that's saying a lot."

She didn't care that the skydiving instructors were gawking at them. She didn't care that her cheeks were windblown, or that her hair was a disheveled mess. She raised her chin and brushed her lips against his.

Jack kissed her back. Hard. Fierce. Hungry.

He grasped her slender shoulders in both hands, touching her, caressing her, making sure she was all right. His blood boiled liked candy syrup, thick and hot. He felt free, weightless, invincible. He'd faced his fear and survived. Survived the jump, survived telling CeeCee the truth, survived his own adventure. He'd done something even his twin brother had never done.

He had tumbled eleven thousand feet from the sky for CeeCee's love.

He held the moment close to his heart, creating a cherished memory.

Their audience applauded.

They didn't care.

"Am I forgiven?" He pulled back, his eyes searching hers.

"Absolutely." She kissed him again.

Someone, he thought it might have been the massive Tiny, snickered.

"I love you, CeeCee."

She fingered his lips. "I love you, too, Jack. So much it scares me."

"Don't be scared. I don't love lightly, but when I do, I'm in it for the long haul. Saying that, I've got to ask you something important." He was afraid to ask the question, but if he'd learned nothing this afternoon, he'd learned to meet his fears head-on.

"Okay."

"Are you sure it's me you love, and not Zack?"

"I never even met Zack! How could I love him?"

"He's funnier than I am, wilder, more adventuresome. He's sexier, too."

"Oh, I don't know about that," she murmured low in her throat. "You're pretty darned sexy, Dr. Travis. And don't forget romantic. Rose petals and champagne and carriage rides and chocolate-covered strawberries."

"But I thought you didn't like my romantic gestures."

"I liked them! Too much. That was the problem. I

was trying to keep up my guard, but you kept slipping in under my radar. You're a tough one to thwart, Jack."

"And you're a tough cookie to romance, sweetheart." He leaned his forehead against hers and peered deeply into her eyes. She saw her future in those dark depths, warm, welcoming, accepting. The intensity of his feelings blew her away. "I promise, CeeCee, I'm here for you. I'll always be here. You don't ever have to worry about me leaving. Face it. I'm a forever kind of guy."

"Oh, Jack," she whispered, tears of joy springing to her eyes.

In that moment, CeeCee Adams knew the truth. She was not cursed, jinxed, hexed, or doomed. She was charmed, enchanted, blessed and redeemed by the love of a wonderful man who'd risked everything to prove to her life was what you made it. There was no such thing as curses. No whammies, no spells, no magic except the power of love.

"Come on," he said and took her hand. "Let's go home."

❧ 17 ❧

This time, she was going to make love to Jack. Really, truly make love with the man of her dreams. And indulge her naughty, secret fantasy.

They were sitting in the whirlpool, warm bubbles surrounding them, a glass of champagne in their hands, toasting themselves and their bravery. They had posted a bogus Out of Order sign on the door and locked it tight against the other apartment dwellers.

Jack had shaved off his beard, and he looked breathtakingly handsome. They were laughing and giddy, still high on their new experiences, their fresh expressions of love.

And they were completely naked, their clothes in a heap beside the hot tub.

CeeCee ran her hands over his smooth chin, happy to have her clean-shaven man back. His tan had started to fade, and he'd gained back the five pounds he'd lost, nicely filling out his muscular frame. He was Dr. Travis again.

Except for that lingering gleam in his dark eyes. Somewhere between playacting his twin and jumping out of that plane, he had developed his own wild streak. He was no longer afraid of adventure, and she was no longer afraid to love. Together, because of each other, they had conquered their fears and won.

At long last she had found true love, but best of all, she knew she would be able to keep it forever.

"I'm so happy it's you I'm in love with and not Zack," she whispered.

"Me, too." His voice was husky with emotion.

"And I can't believe I'm about to make love in a hot tub."

"It's my first time, too," he smiled at her. "But first, there's something we have to do."

"What's that?"

"Give me your hand." She extended her arm across the tub.

"No, the other one."

She switched out. He unclasped the charm bracelet from around her wrist and tossed it beside their towels. "You won't be needing that anymore."

"Satisfied?" She grinned.

"Not totally satisfied. Not yet." Resting in the soothing water, watching CeeCee through half-lidded eyes, sent Jack's thoughts tumbling back to the night before and whet his appetite for more of the same.

Water glistened on her smooth, bare skin. Her damp hair lay draped over her shoulders, framing the tops of her breasts. He grew hard. So hard he felt it straight to his brain.

Lord, she was incredible.

Steam rose up around them. He stretched his foot across the length of the tub and ran his big toe along the bottom of her foot. She giggled.

"What are you doing way over there?"

He was light-headed. High on champagne and CeeCee's intoxicating presence. She smiled that bouncy, flirty smile of hers then coyly stuck out her tongue before ducking her head and denying him access to his favorite part of her. The window to her soul, the mirror of her heart, those stupendous ocean-green eyes.

"Would you like for me to come closer?" She peered at him from lowered lashes.

"Oh, yeah." *In the worst way!*

Laughing lightly, she inched toward him, her champagne flute raised to avoid the churning bubbles. Her laughter sent him into a sensory overload. He loved that laugh. Wanted to hear it ringing in his head for the rest of his life.

"How about here?" she asked. "Is this near enough?'

"Closer," he murmured, feeling very, very lusty.

She scooted nearer. "Here?"

"Closer."

"You sound dangerous." Her eyes twinkled, enjoying the game they were playing. He liked the game, too. Jack hadn't felt this free, this lighthearted since he was a teenager.

He crooked a finger at her. "All the better to eat you with, my dear."

She giggled again and covered her mouth with a delicate hand.

"I think you've had too much champagne," he diagnosed.

"Only one glass." She smiled smugly and raised a finger.

"You're a cheap date if one glass of champagne does you in."

"Not drunk," she proclaimed. "A little tipsy maybe, but definitely not drunk."

"You're an incredible woman."

"How so?" She arched an eyebrow.

"You're a dream come true."

"So are you."

He slid his tongue past her lips. Her laughter dissipated.

She tasted so good! Like champagne and honey and heat. He kissed her. Hard and long and thoroughly.

"Wow," she murmured when he broke the kiss. "Wow."

"Just call me Dr. Love."

"Well, medicine man." She reached out for his hand and tucked it between her legs. Jack's heart leapfrogged. "I've got this ache. Right here. Have you got a remedy?"

"Have I got a remedy!" He pulled her smack-dab onto his lap. Her thighs straddled his. "You tell me," his voice grew husky. "Do I have the cure for what ails you, sweetheart?"

"Oh my!" Her fingers searched for his arousal and wrapped around him.

"Uh." Jack grunted at the intensity of the sensation. He cupped the soft curves of her bottom in both hands and tugged her closer.

Her breasts bobbed above the water, shimmering with wetness, her nipples sweetly puckered. Jack lowered his head, placed his mouth over first one pink straining nipple and then the other. Her hands went to his shoulders, her fingernails digging lightly into his flesh as she moaned with pleasure.

She bumped against him with her pelvis. "My ache, Dr. Love, it's getting worse. You better do something. Quick."

"I'm a doctor who likes to take my time."

He watched a trail of perspiration trickle between her breasts. He licked it, savoring the saltiness of her heated skin. He lowered his hand, came up behind her bottom, and slowly began to stroke her between her firm, supple thighs.

She made soft keening noises that told him she was winding up to something incredible.

"Make love to me, Jack. Now. Right now," she pleaded.

Happy to oblige, he got a condom from the pocket of his discarded jeans and slipped it on. He lifted her higher in the water and up onto his bludgeoning erection, sliding deep into her sweetness. She hissed in her breath. Jack closed his eyes, relishing the glory of their joining, relishing CeeCee.

"Kiss me," she commanded.

He roamed his mouth over hers, sucking, licking, reveling in her warm moistness. He slipped his tongue inside, feeling the rough edges of her teeth, tasting the wine's tart sweetness.

She moaned, then leaned back, breaking their kiss. He held on to her with both hands wrapped securely around her waist. She moved over him, using her knees as a fulcrum to deepen his penetration.

They soared together on the wildest of roller-coaster rides, lurching steadily higher and higher, anticipating what was coming next, knowing there would be a frantic plunge, hurtling down into ecstasy as they climaxed together in one powerful shudder. Jack finally floated down from the nether reaches of passion, his breathing hard, his mind scrambled.

She lay draped over him, her face buried against his neck, her wet hair sticking to her face. From the waist up they were drenched in sweat. From the waist down, they were drained.

"I love you, CeeCee Adams." Jack hitched in a breath, amazed at what he'd managed to accomplish in spite of himself. He'd won this woman over, freed her from her past, made it okay for her to love. He was so proud of her.

"And I love you, Jack."

He kissed her once, twice, three times. Her eyes drifted closed. The pulse beating at the hollow of her throat perfectly matched the rhythm of his heart.

She wanted him. He, Jack Travis, and not his twin brother. No more pretenses, no more deception.

He kissed that supple neck, ran his tongue along that pounding pulse.

"I love your hair. It's wild and free, spilling over

your shoulders like a waterfall of fireworks. Wild and free like you." A terrifying thought suddenly occurred to him. "I don't want my love to change you, to pin you down."

"You won't," she said fiercely, wrapping her arms around his neck. "I only acted wild and free because I thought that's all I could ever have. I never thought I'd be lucky enough to find my anchor. A man who isn't buffeted off course by life's storms."

"But anchors can drag people down."

"Jack, darling, listen to me. I've spent my whole life longing for someone to ground me, and that's exactly what you do. We balance each other. I'm air, you're earth. You keep me steady, I lift you up."

She was right. So very right.

She inspired him to greater heights, to try things he would never undertake on his own. She lifted his heart, his soul, his mind. He peered into those laughing green eyes. She completed him and made him whole in the way nothing else ever had. He was her harbor, and she was indeed the wind beneath his wings.

And at long last, they'd both found their way home.

EPILOGUE

"I found a way to reverse the fortuneteller's curse," Jack said.

They were walking hand in hand on a secluded stretch of beach in Galveston, the evening sun sliding its way west, a full moon rising in the east.

"Oh?"

"Guaranteed."

"But you said there was no such thing as the Jessup family whammy, remember?"

The last six months together had been perfect, idyllic. She trusted Jack, with all her heart and soul, but what if something happened that was out of their control? Giving up a lifetime indoctrination was difficult, and she was still working her head around the reality that she was living a fairy tale and all her dreams were coming to pass.

"Yes, sweetheart, but you've believed in the whammy for so long I figured a little exorcism ritual was in order."

How did he know exactly what to say? She did need some sort of ritual, some sense of closure in order to shut the door on the past forever.

"So where did you get your information?" She slanted him a coy glance.

"I have my sources."

"This wouldn't have anything to do with the Romanian woman whose baby you delivered last week during your obstetrical rotation, would it?" she teased.

"It might." His grin widened.

He stopped on a rock pier and pulled her into his arms just as the sun plunked down on the horizon. The wind ruffled their hair; the air smelled crisp and sharp. They were all alone, no one else in sight.

"So what's involved?"

"It's a two-step process."

"It is?"

"Yep."

"So what's step number one?"

"I'm way ahead of you on that one. First, you take a negative talisman."

"A what?"

"You know, something that represents the negative experience. In this case, your anticharm bracelet."

"Oh." CeeCee wrapped a hand around her bare wrist. She hadn't missed the bracelet since Jack had taken it from her the day they'd made love in the hot tub.

"Anyway, you take the negative talisman and use it to make a positive one."

"I'm not following you."

Jack's eyes twinkled and he pulled something from his pocket. A small black box. He cracked it open, and CeeCee stared down at an exquisite two-carat diamond ring.

"I had your bracelet melted down and used the gold to make the setting for your engagement ring. The diamond came from my grandmother. She and Grandpa were married sixty years. My parents have been married thirty-five. Long and happy marriages run in my family, CeeCee, so my history cancels out yours. This ring symbolizes the death of old superstitions and the beginning of our new life together."

She raised a hand to her throat, her heart galloping a thousand miles a minute. "Oh, Jack."

He knelt on the rock beside her and took her left hand in his. "CeeCee Adams, will you do me the honor of becoming my wife?"

"Are you sure?" she whispered. "That it's really me you want?"

"None other, sweetheart. Until death do us part. Please say yes." He looked so earnestly endearing, so full of hope and promise.

The sun had disappeared, but the moon had risen higher. Her stomach clutched. She wavered there in moonlight, the surf crashing into the rocks. She could choose fear, or she could choose freedom.

All it took was one little word.

How could she say no to this man? The one who'd loved her enough to pretend to be his twin in order to win her. The one who'd jumped from a plane to prove his love. The one who promised to stand by her through thick and thin, no matter what came. The one who'd so thoughtfully gone to all this trouble to fashion a very special engagement ring for her.

And how could she say no when saying yes felt so incredibly right?

"Yes," she said. "Yes, Jack, I'll marry you."

"Oh, CeeCee." He gathered her closer and rained kisses on her face. "I'm going to spend the rest of my life showing you how much I love you."

For a long time, they simply kissed, enjoying the moment, enjoying each other, then CeeCee pulled away and angled her head up at him.

"Wait a minute. You said breaking the curse was a two-step process. What's number two?"

"It's going to be a sacrifice on my part." He laughed. "It requires me to be adventuresome, free-spirited and spontaneous."

"What is it!" she demanded.

"You sure you want to know?"

"The curse won't be lifted until we do this thing, right?"

"That's correct." He grinned.

"So give it up, Dr. Travis, and stop with all the mystery. What must we do?"

"We must make wild, passionate love on the beach under a full moon and say goodbye to my bachelorhood."

"Really?" she purred.

"Really," he said. "We could start tonight and finish on our honeymoon in Hawaii."

"What!" she squealed.

He pulled two tickets from his shirt pockets and grinning, he passed them over to her.

"You were pretty sure of yourself," she said, lovingly fingering the tickets to paradise.

"Sure enough to count on you, sweetheart."

"Well then, what are we waiting for?"

And so they made love under the full moon on the deserted beach, once and for all putting an end to the Jessup family whammy and in the process, ensuring themselves a very long and happy future.

DEAR READER,

Readers are an author's life blood and the stories couldn't happen without *you*. Thank you so much for reading. I do appreciate more than you could ever know!

As a nurse for twenty-two years, I brought my medical knowledge to this series and it was such fun using my background in the telling of these stories.

If you enjoyed *The Jinx*, I would so appreciate a review. You have no idea how much your input means to an author.

You can check out all the books in the Heart-throb Hospital series here.

Don't miss the third book in the series, *The Hotshot*, where Janet falls for the absolute wrong guy.

If you'd like to keep up with my latest releases, you can sign up for my newsletter @ https://loriwilde.com/subscribe/ Or follow me on Bookbub.

To check out my other books, you can visit me on the web @ www.loriwilde.com.

Much love and light!

—Lori

From the moment Dr. Bennett Sheridan stepped into the operating suite at Saint Madeleine's University Hospital, his freshly scrubbed hands held up in front of him and a toothpaste-commercial grin breaking across his cover-model face, Lacy Calder was a grade-A, number-one goner.

She glanced up from where she stood perched on her step stool spreading autoclaved instruments across the sterile field, preparing for an upcoming coronary bypass surgery, when she turned her head and saw him standing inside the doorway.

Her heart gave a crazy bump against her chest, and her breath crawled from her lungs. Never in all her twenty-seven years had she experienced such an immediate reaction to anyone.

It was intense and undeniable.

Endorphins collided with adrenaline. Sex hormones twisted in her lower abdomen like a paint bucket in a shaker. Excitement, approval, and sheer joy sprinted through Lacy's nerve endings as fast as electrical impulses skipping along telephone lines, wiring urgent messages to her brain.

It's him! It's the Thunderbolt.

Oh, my goodness gracious, Great-Gramma Kahonachek was right. He wasn't some silly myth like Bigfoot or the Loch Ness Monster or the Tooth Fairy. Lacy was not the sort of woman who lusted diligently after complete strangers, and yet she was lusting after this one.

Big-time.

Step aside, McDreamy! Beat it, Doug Ross! Take a Hike, House! Move over, Dr. Dorian! Dr. Bennett Sheridan has arrived!

The man's Mr. Universe physique begged her to caress him with her eyes. He was tall, well over six feet, and broad-shouldered. He wore green hospital scrubs, but the normally shapeless garment seemed to actually enhance his amazing body.

With his arms curled upward, still damp from the mandatory fifteen-minute surgical scrub, she could see the hard ridges of his biceps bulging beneath thin cotton sleeves.

He possessed spiced peach skin as dark as an itinerant beachcomber's, and a firmly muscled neck spoke of time spent pursuing outdoor athletic activities. A tennis player, she decided, or maybe softball. His nose, crooked slightly to the right, announced that it had been broken sometime in the past, giving him a tough, no-nonsense air.

A fight, she wondered, or perhaps an accident?

His teeth, straight and white, flashed like a linen sail behind his widening smile. An accompanying dimple carved a beguiling hole into his right cheek. When his chocolate-kisses eyes met hers, Dr. Feel Good made it seem as if she were the only woman on the face of the earth.

Be still, my heart.

She felt an unmistakable "click," as if something very important had settled into place. Something that, until now, had been sorely out of kilter and she'd never known it.

At long last *it* had happened.

Lacy's knees turned to water. Her pulse hammered, and her tongue stuck to the roof of her mouth as surely as if plastered there by creamy peanut butter.

"Morning, ladies," he greeted Lacy and the circulating nurse, Pam Marks. "I'm Dr. Bennett Sheridan, third-year resident on a study fellowship from Boston

General. I'll be interning with Dr. Laramie for the next six weeks."

They had known he was coming on board, of course. Dr. Laramie had made a point of bragging about the fine young doctor, summa cum laude from Harvard, who'd flown to Houston specifically to study under him.

A young doctor who'd beaten out three hundred other anxious applicants for the prestigious opportunity. What Lacy hadn't expected was that Dr. Sheridan would melt her heart with that let's-break-open-a-bottle-of-champagne smile or that she would experience the most desperate urge to razzle-dazzle him.

But how could she ever hope to impress a man so obviously out of her league? He was Mike Trout. She was the water girl.

His gaze landed on her and stuck.

A long, weighted moment passed.

Lacy gulped. Fully gowned and masked as she was, her hair covered with a sky-blue surgical cap and her feet slippered in matching shoe covers, Lacy couldn't help wondering why he stared so intently. Had she forgotten to put eye shadow on one eye? Did she have a smudge on her forehead? Was her mascara smeared?

Just her luck to meet the man of her dreams on the day she'd flubbed Makeup Application 101.

Unnerved, Lacy took a step backward and promptly somersaulted off her stool.

Clay

Jonah

ABOUT THE AUTHOR

Lori Wilde s the New York Times, USA Today, and Publishers Weekly bestselling author of ninety-one works of romantic fiction. Her books have been translated into twenty-six languages, with more than six million copies sold worldwide. Her breakout novel, The First Love Cookie Club, has been optioned for a TV movie as has her Wedding Veil Wishes series. Lori is a registered nurse with a BSN from Texas Christian University.

Made in the USA
Columbia, SC
17 October 2020